one tree hill

The Beginning

By Jenny Markas

Based in part on "One Tree Hill: Pilot,"
by Mark Schwahn

SCHOLASTIC INC.

New York   Toronto   London   Auckland   Sydney
Mexico City   New Delhi   Hong Kong   Buenos Aires

ISBN 0-439-71560-1

Designed by Louise Bova
Printed in the U.S.A.

First printing, January 2005
12 11 10 9 8 7 6 5 4 3 2 1   5 6 7 8 9 10/0

Prologue

It's a glorious day. The library windows, cracked open to let in the fresh, crisp air, face out on the Tree Hill High School quad, where three venerable sycamores stretch bare limbs to a clear blue December sky. It's the kind of day that makes you want to take off, hike the nearest mountain, fling open your arms to the world. Or something.

Where do you *not* want to be? Study hall. Until exactly eleven minutes after one, that is. A moment nobody who's in that room will ever forget. A moment that separates "before" from "after."

Just as the minute hand clicks past the two on the big clock over the door, Coach Durham — known as Whitey to every mother's son in Tree Hill, North Carolina — strides into the room.

"Scott!" he shouts.

Two heads turn in his direction.

One, darkly handsome and held high with a self-confidence bordering on arrogance.

The other, with golden waves framing a sensitive face and eyes that might have belonged to a fox struggling to escape from a trap.

"'Sup, Coach?" asks the dark boy, Nathan. He begins to pile his books together, getting ready to head to the gym. No doubt Whitey wants to talk to him about how the Ravens will handle defense in Friday's game.

"Not you," Whitey answers brusquely. He nods to the other boy, the blond. "You."

By now, everyone in the room is staring. At Whitey. At Nathan.

At Lucas.

Nathan is still looking at Whitey. His mouth hangs open. Whitey's eyes meet Nathan's with an even gaze. "You read a book or something," Whitey tells him. Then he turns on his heel and leaves the room, not even checking to see if Lucas is following.

Slowly, Lucas gathers his things. Stands up. Darts a look at Nathan. And follows Whitey out of the room.

PART I

Summer Storms

June 15

I'm seein' it all through a haze —
Moonlit nights and morning rays
But I'm too beat, too long on my feet
Workin' my way
Through the dog days
Of summer. . . .

Notes to self: finish bridge.
E minor?
Country blues à la Lucinda Williams.

lyric fragment, Haley's songwriting notebook

"What can I get you, ma'am?" Haley notices that it's already taking every ounce of patience she can muster just to sound marginally pleasant. Not a good sign, considering that she's only three hours into her first day of work. But not all that surprising, considering that it's the very first day of summer vacation and Haley didn't even get to sleep in.

It's not like her shift started first thing in the morning. The Dog Kart, thankfully, is not open for breakfast. After all, nobody in their right mind would eat a chili dog before eleven, would they? (Haley has a nasty suspicion that there are plenty of folks out there who would.) But Pete, her boss, insisted on her showing up by nine A.M. for a "uniform check." Which meant that Haley had, oh, approximately eighteen hours — from the moment she walked out of school to the moment she put on her Dog Kart apron and hat — to enjoy her summer.

Once the uniform went on, it was all over.

How to describe Pete's twisted sense of humor and bizarre ideas about marketing? Wasn't it enough that the apron was a hideous, unflattering coverall featuring the Dog Kart logo in shades of neon green and yellow? Apparently not. Apparently Pete's sensibilities were not satisfied until he'd designed the ultimate humiliation: the Dog Kart hat. It started with a normal-looking baseball cap (avec neon-yellow bill, of course). But the logo alone wasn't enough. Instead, the cap features a stuffed dog, some sort of brown, vaguely dachshundy-looking thing, its long snout and floppy ears sticking out to the left and its long behind and whippy tail sticking out to the right. The effect is sort of like one of those arrow-through-the-head gags — except with a dog.

Ouch.

Five dollars and fifteen cents an hour is not nearly enough, Haley thinks for the thousandth time, as the snot-nosed little kid at the window pulls at his mother's hand and, giggling wildly, points at the dog bisecting Haley's head. "Look, Mommy, that lady has a dog through her brain!"

"What can I get you, ma'am?" Haley repeats tiredly, ignoring the boy.

The mother, one of those perfectly coiffed, Mercedes SUV-driving soccer moms from up on the Hill, frowns. Haley can tell she's pissed because Haley isn't playing along with her precious son. Haley doesn't care. Pencil poised, she waits for the order. What'll it be this time? Perhaps the Dogtacular, which features a corn dog, a chili dog, fries, and nachos with chili? Nah. The soccer mom would never be seen chowing on the Kart's most heinous special. She'll just get a plain dog for the boy, hold the bun so she's not tempted by the carbs.

"Just a hot dog."

No "please," Haley notices. Not that she expected one.

"And a little cup of ketchup on the side."

Haley doesn't bother to point out that there's ketchup on the counter. She just turns to grab a dog off the rollers. The smell is nauseating in the small, enclosed trailer. Haley is strongly considering becoming a vegan.

When she turns back, Haley's stomach sinks. The situation has just gone from barely tolerable to something three steps beyond that.

A '63 Comet has pulled into the Kart's crunchy gravel parking lot. Tank-sized, black with a white hardtop, dripping with chrome, and blasting the Ramones' "I Wanna Be Sedated," the vintage car is immediately recognizable to every citizen in Tree Hill. So is its driver, a petite, stunning blond with cascading ringlets, a quirky-sweet smile, and a killer bod. Peyton Sawyer, cheerleader deluxe.

Piling out behind Peyton are her basketball-hero boyfriend, Nathan Scott — Tree Hill's answer to Michael Jordan — and her bud Brooke, also a cheerleader, the brunette edition.

"Oh, god," Haley moans under her breath. Just when she thought it couldn't get any worse. She wishes she could tear off the stupid hat, but Pete is right behind her, changing the grease in the fry-o-later.

"What?" asks the soccer mom.

"That'll be one sixty-five," Haley says, holding out her hand.

The woman pays and leaves.

Meanwhile, Peyton and Nathan are lounging against the picnic table, staring up at the menu sign. Their arms are entwined, their hips pressed together. They consult in whispers about what to order. Then Nathan turns to face Peyton, tips up her chin with a finger, and they kiss. And kiss again.

Get a room, Haley thinks, even more nauseated by this than by the smell of frying dogs.

Brooke approaches the window, weaving a little, and leans in, so close that Haley can smell the unmistakable odor of Mike's Hard Lemonade on her breath. It's not even four o'clock yet, and Brooke's already been drinking. Here's to summer vacation!

Brooke flashes one of her dimply smiles, the one she usually reserves for boys. Then she turns back to Peyton and Nathan and starts humming under her breath. Haley recognizes the tune, even before Brooke starts singing the words. "How Much Is That Doggie in the Window," Brooke croons, giggling at her own wit.

She keeps at it the whole time they're there, switching from "You Ain't Nothin' But a Hound Dog," to "Who Let the Dogs Out," and back to "How Much Is That Doggie. . . ."

Haley does her best to ignore it, but she knows her face is flaming. She notices that Peyton tries to hush Brooke, probably more because her half-wrecked friend is embarrassing her than out of any sense of decency toward Haley. Nathan barely seems to notice what's going on; he's so into Peyton he doesn't register anything else. As far as Haley can tell, Brooke, Peyton, and Nathan don't even recognize her. That's how it is at Tree Hill: The Hill folks inhabit a whole other world from the river rats like Haley. The geography of the town just seems to lend itself to those differences. Plus, other than school, there just aren't that many places the two groups mix. It's not like Prince Nathan, whose father owns the biggest car dealership in town, is ever going to be working at the Dog Kart. Or anywhere else that pays minimum wage.

Haley knows she isn't a dog. Her looks, in her own clear-eyed assessment, are more than adequate. She may not be as blond as Peyton, or as curvy as Brooke, but she's no monster. She has a nice, open face, decent wavy brown hair, and a body she's not ashamed to show off at the local swimming hole. But she's no Hill girl, and she never will be. Haley's never had a pedicure or a massage, never been given her mom's credit card and sent to the mall, never had her hair colored "just for fun." Nor would she want to do any of those things. She digs shopping at Do It Again, the local vintage thrift shop. Her hair color is fine as it is. And she can put nail polish on all by herself, thank you very much.

Still, it rankles. It's like Brooke doesn't even see her as a girl, just as an object to make fun of.

Finally, finally, they leave, peeling out in the Comet. Peyton drives like a demon, always zero to sixty in seconds. She screeches right past a basketball-dribbling figure jogging toward the Kart, and her head doesn't even turn to notice the pedestrian she's almost creamed.

The pedestrian notices her, though. And Haley notices him noticing. "Didn't think you were into blonds," she says lightly, as her oldest, bestest bud approaches the window.

"Hey, dawg," Lucas replies, looking at her hat.

She laughs. At least he has the decency to make fun of her to her face. She and Lucas have teased each other and loved each other — like brother and sister — for how many years now? Too many to count. Haley inserted herself into his tiny family — it's just him and his mom, Karen — way back when she was wearing size-three OshKosh B'Gosh overalls. Haley is the youngest in a huge family and her house is always chaotic. It always seemed so much saner at Lucas's house, with just the two of them.

"All done over at Keith's?" she asks as she fetches a corn dog and fries for Lucas. He works at his uncle's auto body shop, and not just in the summer. Lucas and Karen need every cent they can both earn just to get by.

Lucas nods. "I'm on my way to the court. Just stopped in to fuel up." He bites into his dog.

Lucas spends every spare minute shooting basketball at the beat-up outdoor court down by the river. Haley knows how much he loves the place and his posse there, the guys he plays with. *Funny*, she thinks. *It's like Lucas went looking for a big family the same way I went looking for a little one.*

"Breakfast of champions," Haley says, giving a little shiver as she watches the corn dog disappear. Then the dinner rush starts, and she barely has a chance to wave good-bye to Lucas before she's swept into a flood of orders.

*　　*　　*

Peyton screeches to a stop in front of Brooke's house. "Later," she calls as Brooke stumbles up the path.

"What is with that chick?" Nathan asks as they tear off again.

"She's not 'that chick,'" Peyton says frostily. "She's my friend. And she's just celebrating because summer is here." She glances over at Nathan while she waits impatiently for a light to turn green. How did he end up in her car? Sometimes it still seems surreal. For so long, she'd held out against the stereotype. So what if she was the prettiest cheerleader in school, and Nathan was the handsome star basketball player? Was it, like, predetermined that they had to go out? Peyton wasn't buying it. Instead, she dated guys like Mark Sutter, who collects original punk music on vinyl, and Brian Estleman, who plays drums in this band called Uterus. Her friends thought she was nuts.

Finally, something clicked. It happened at a

postgame party, naturally. Peyton was sitting by herself, avoiding the crush of jocks around the keg. Maroon 5 was on the stereo: "She Will Be Loved." Suddenly, there he was, looming over her with two cups of keg beer. Nathan Scott, all charming smiles and sincere eye contact. "Drink?" he asked, sitting down next to her on the couch. She took the beer. She drank it. They kissed. Oh, yeah. She was lost.

Nathan might be arrogant. He might be self-centered. He might be single-mindedly obsessed with basketball. He might even be egotistical.

(In fact, there's no "might" about it. He is all those things and more.)

But Nathan also has the softest lips and the hardest pecs of any boy Peyton has ever kissed. And this way of looking at her with this I'm-a-little-lost-puppy expression that goes straight to her heart.

And a beach house, which will be very handy this summer.

So what if he doesn't like the same kind of music? Or even know who The Microphones are?

So what if he doesn't even have a clue that what she loves most is drawing?

So what if he forgets to call her when he's hanging out with his buddies, immersed in some epic PlayStation battle?

"Peyton?" Nathan snaps his fingers in her face. "Why are you staring at me that way? And I don't know if you've noticed, but there've been, like, three green lights since we've been sitting here."

"Whatever," Peyton says, throwing the car into drive and taking off before she even checks what color the light is. "I was just thinking."

"About giving me a back rub?" Nathan asks, sliding a hand onto her thigh.

That's kind of a code. Things usually started with a back rub, but they rarely ended there.

"Are your parents home?" she asks, giving him a sidelong glance.

"Dad is. My mom's away on business, as usual," Nathan answers. "How about your place?"

"Fine," says Peyton, knowing her dad's away for the weekend. It isn't like she and Nathan have a lot to talk about, anyway. Might as well get some other activities in.

Down at the river court, Lucas and the guys are still tossing it around, even though they can barely see the ball. Somebody threw a rock at one of the court lights a week or so ago, and the city hasn't gotten around to fixing it yet.

Mouth is on the sidelines, along with Edwards. They don't actually play much; they're more into narrating the game for the thousands of invisible fans that exist only in their twisted brains. "Luke is on fire tonight," Mouth reports, holding up a rolled magazine as a pretend mic. "Skills can't seem to get the ball away no matter what he does."

"You're not kidding, Mouth," Edwards chimes in, leaning toward the magazine. It's a low-budget show: They share a mic. "Skills isn't his usual self tonight, that much is clear. Even Fergie is shooting better than he is."

"You guys are harsh!" yells Junk from the court. "Everybody has an off night."

"Except you," Mouth calls back. "You're having an off year."

Skills doesn't even seem to hear the banter. He does seem to be lagging, Lucas notices. He decides to take it easy on the guy, but two seconds later Lucas has abandoned that plan. He can't resist driving to the basket for a layup when Skills falls for a left fake.

Mouth and Edwards supply appropriate fan noises, cheering wildly for the play.

"Must be that corn dog I ate," Lucas reports, rubbing his stomach. "Nothing like a supernutritious meal to set you up for success."

"Ah, the Dog Kart," says Edwards. "The place to see and be seen."

"No kidding," says Lucas. "Even the Hill people show up there."

"Oh?" asks Junk, raising one eyebrow. Nobody loves gossip more than Junk Moretti. "Who'd you spot downing chili dogs?"

Lucas shrugs. "You know, just, like, Nathan Scott and that chick he hangs out with —"

"Peyton Sawyer," Junk supplies.

"I guess," Lucas says, though he knows very well that's who it is. Everybody knows Peyton. But he feels the need to hide the fact that something about Peyton just . . . gets to him. It bugs him, too. She's so unattainable, so Hilly, so not his type. Why does seeing her always seem to shake him up a little?

"You guess," Junk says, noticing the way Lucas is suddenly looking down at the ground. "Don't even go there," he advises. "That girl will never look at a river rat like you."

"What are you talking about?" Lucas asks, tossing him the ball. "C'mon, let's play. Is this a ball game or a slumber party?"

Junk catches the ball and dribbles it toward the basket, unsuccessfully hiding a sly smile.

"King me," Lucas says, an hour or so later. He and Karen are on the front porch, sipping lemonade and playing checkers. It's a summer tradition for the two of them. ". . . And — gotcha!" Lucas announces, hopscotching his king through Karen's entire army of pieces.

"What does that make it," asks Keith, coming up the walk with a brown paper bag under his arm, "a thousand to nine-ninety-nine?"

"Eight thirty-one to eight twenty-four," Lucas corrects him, after checking the pad next to the board. They've kept track, all these years.

Keith sits down on the top step. "Beer?" he asks Karen, pulling a six-pack of beer out of the bag.

"I'm set," she says, holding up her lemonade. "There's plenty of this," she adds, "if you'd rather." There's a certain tightness in her voice. She and Keith are close, and she worries about his drinking. Not that he's some falling-down drunk, but there's no denying he tips a few too many now and then.

Lucas hears it, too, and shoots a glance at Karen. He hates it when she gets on Keith's case. If she could just relax and accept the guy for who he is, maybe someday he'd be more than just Lucas's uncle and a good pal who's there to help when the plumbing breaks. Lucas has often thought that he wouldn't actually mind that too much. It's not that he misses having a dad — he's pretty used to it, since he's never known any other life — but Keith is a good guy and for the most part he seems to make Karen happy. More than anything, Lucas would like to see his mom be happy.

"I'm beat," Lucas says now. "Take my place, Keith? Defend male supremacy?"

Karen snorts.

Keith swings into Lucas's seat.

And Lucas goes up to turn on his computer and surf the Net — at least till he's checked out Peyton's webcam site.

Nathan doesn't get home until about one A.M. He slips in through the kitchen door, pauses to stand in front of the fridge and guzzle some milk from the carton, then starts to tiptoe upstairs — only to hear his dad call out from the den.

"First day of summer, and you stay out all night? That's not how it's gonna be," Dan says. He sits in his easy chair, remote in one hand and a glass of whiskey in the other.

Nathan looks at him. Suddenly, out of nowhere, a

word pops into his mind: *lonely*. He shakes it off. It's true his mom is never home, but he doesn't like thinking of his dad as some pathetic loser. Not that anyone could ever think of Dan Scott that way. Successful businessman, sports hero . . . There wasn't a person in Tree Hill over thirty who didn't remember Dan Scott's amazing abilities on the basketball court. He could definitely have gone pro, probably would have if Nathan hadn't come along when he did.

"I was just out with Peyton," he says.

"Look, Nathan," Dan says, putting the drink down and leaning forward, all intensity. "Don't you get it? Champions are made in the off-season. Just because you don't have a game this week doesn't mean you can let up on your workouts. Your career depends on it. If you have a good season this year, the scouts will be flocking to this town like bees to honey." He fishes into a paper bag on the floor beside his chair. "I got you this," he says, handing Nathan a blank training diary with a picture of Scottie Pippen on the front.

"Um, thanks," says Nathan.

"I don't want to have to set a curfew for you," Dan says. "Keep track of what you do every day: shooting practice, sprints, weight work. If you're putting in the time, I'll give you as much freedom as you need. Deal?"

Nathan hangs his head. "But what about Peyton?" he asks, trying not to sound whiny. Dan hates whining. "We have plans —"

Dan cuts him off.

"Girls are great," Dan says. "In moderation. You just have to be really careful not to spend too much time or energy on them."

"Like you did with that girl you knocked up in high school?" Nathan blurts out.

Dan's eyes flash, and the conversation comes to a dead end. Nathan has entered the danger zone, and he knows it. Nobody talks about that. Nobody ever talks about that.

About the son Dan fathered, just after his senior year at Tree Hill High. About how the kid lives right across town, with the mother who brought him up all by herself after Dan took off and went to college. But at the same time, it's no secret. Nathan saw the guy today, that loser who came dribbling his ratty old ball into the Dog Kart just as he and Peyton and Brooke were leaving. Nathan's seen him in school. Nathan knows where he works — at Dan's brother Keith's body shop. Nathan's heard that he shoots hoops down at the river court, with the rest of the rats. Nathan even knows the boy's name. He never says it out loud, rarely even says it to himself. But he knows it.

Lucas.

Lucas Scott.

His brother.

July 4

Okay, Ms. Stevenson, you wanted a summer diary, you got one. You said anything goes and that I'll get that missing English credit as long as I hand in at least 20 pages. Here goes: So far, this summer has been da bomb. My tan is coming along beautifully (Note: No bikini-top lines). I've been extremely careful to avoid dehydration. And my — ahem — "love life" is alive and totally kickin'. So far this summer I've made out with 7 (seven) boys (see attached list). Now, however, I have my eye on a MAN!

entry, Brooke's summer diary (for credit)

"Pass me the Poison," says Peyton, holding out a hand.

Brooke reaches across the bed and hands over

a small bottle of dark green nail polish. Peyton examines it. "I don't know," she says. "Nathan'll probably think this is too, like, alt."

"Why, just because it looks like something Marilyn Manson would wear?" Brooke asks snidely. "I'm with Nathan. Stick to this one, what's it called? Pretty in Pink? Or maybe Very Berry. I'm sorry, but green toenails are just kinda —" She makes a gagging noise. Then she goes back to painting her own toenails, using a shade of scarlet called Passion. It matches the lacy underwire bustier she bought earlier that day at the upscale Tree Hill Marketplace, otherwise known as the mall. "I'm hoping Rusty's into red," she muses. "You'd think he would be, with that name."

"I don't know," Peyton says. "Some redheads hate their hair."

"Who could hate his hair?" Brooke sighs. "It's not, like, that pukey carrot color. It's more like auburn. And so thick. And so wavy. And I am so dying to run my hands through it. . . ." She trails off, and Peyton can tell she's diving back into one of her fantasies.

Brooke has had her eye on this guy Rusty for the last three weeks, ever since she spotted him at Jackson's, the one bar in town known for tolerating even the most amateurish fake IDs. He was shooting pool, and even Peyton had to admit it: He was good at the game, unlike most of the poseur frat boys who hung out there.

Still, he is a frat boy. Old enough to be drinking on his own legally earned license. Old enough to spell trouble for Brooke, Peyton thinks, as she dabs her big toenail with Poison. College guys are never a good idea. Sure, they're entertained by the idea of underage townies, but when it comes down to anything more than some groping and sloppy kisses at a kegger, they're not much use. Plus, they're likely to transfer, flunk out, or meet some girl their own age in Psych 101, and then you never hear from them again. Peyton doesn't actually have firsthand experience with any of this, but she's heard the stories.

So has Brooke.

But she doesn't care. She must have Rusty. "Remember how his butt looked when he was leaning over the pool table for that corner shot?" she asks dreamily. Her hand slips and she paints a good portion of her big toe bright red. "Shoot," she says, jumping up and hopping over to the bedside table for the nail polish remover.

"I remember," Peyton says. "I also remember hearing him cuss and seeing him nearly put a fist through the wall when he missed that same shot."

"So he's got a temper, so what?" Brooke asks. "He's passionate. I like that in a man." She licks her lips and raises her eyebrows, vamping it up. "Plus, it would just be so cool to, like, bring him to the Fall Fling. Picture me walking into the gym in something strapless, with that on my arm."

"Fall Fling is months away," Peyton reminds her friend. "If I know you, Rusty will be a distant memory by then."

Brooke shrugs. "You're probably right. You usually are. Remember when you warned me against going out with David Troutheimer?"

Peyton bursts out laughing. "That was in second

grade!" she says. "And he was already, like, your fourth boyfriend." She shakes her head. "I told you he'd never get serious. He was too into dinosaurs."

"True," Brooke admits, giggling. "He left me for a stegosaurus. Or was it a triceratops? Anyway, it happened just like you predicted it would. One day we were all kissy-face under the jungle gym, and the next he only had eyes for that plastic dino model in Mrs. Brewster's room." She sighs. "Anyway," she goes on, "Rusty's in a whole 'nother league."

"From a second-grader?" Peyton asks. "I should hope so." She rolls over on the bed and reaches for her cell. "What time are we going to meet Nathan?" she asks, snapping it open and hitting one on the speed dial. There's a big Fourth of July celebration down by the river that night: parade, carnival rides, music, fireworks, the whole nine yards. Everybody in Tree Hill will be there.

"Let's get there at eight, for the parade. Fireworks start at nine," Brooke says. "The ones in the sky, that is. If I meet up with Rusty before then, there may be a few on earth, too." She's finished with her toenails by now, and she's pouting into a mirror, adding a fresh layer of pink gloss to her already shiny lips.

Peyton rolls her eyes. "Hey," she says into the phone. "Done with your workout?" She listens. "Cool," she goes on. "I'll pick you up in an hour." She listens again, then giggles. "Maybe," she says. "We'll see." She hangs up.

"Is Nathan getting some tonight?" Brooke asks suggestively.

Peyton blushes a little. "None of your beeswax," she says, giving Brooke a little swat.

"You guys getting along okay?" Brooke asks. "He seemed a little on edge the other night."

"We're fine," Peyton answers. "It's just his dad. You know, he really pressures him. Nathan's supposed to be Mr. Basketball Star, and nothing else is ever going to be good enough."

"Guess Dan's other son is kinda lucky," Brooke says lightly, watching Peyton's face. "I mean, Dan ignores him completely. Maybe that's better." They haven't talked a whole lot about the whole Nathan/Lucas thing. Brooke wonders how Peyton will react.

The one thing she doesn't expect?

The way Peyton blushes when she hears Lucas's name.

Hmmm, thinks Brooke. It's not the first time she's seen Peyton react this way, either. Once, a couple of weeks ago, Peyton made up some excuse to drive by that crappy old basketball court down by the river. A bunch of river rats — including Lucas — were shooting hoops there. Peyton pulled up, and she and Brooke sat there drinking the Frappuccinos they'd just bought and watching for a while — until they were noticed by this guy on the sidelines. He was pretending to be a sportscaster, but he dropped the act as soon as he saw Peyton and Brooke. He actually came over to talk to them. Said his name was Mouth. Brooke thought his name should be Eyes, given the way he couldn't keep his off her chest.

"Do you like him?" Brooke asks outright. Why

waste time beating around the bush with her best friend?

"Who, Lucas? As if!" Peyton tightens the cap on the Poison bottle, carefully avoiding Brooke's eyes. "I'm just kinda, you know, fascinated by the whole thing. You know, how he's actually Nathan's brother and all. Well, half brother. But they never talk or interact or anything. Don't you think it's weird?"

Brooke nods. "Yeah," she agrees. "Sad, too. The way his mom had to bring him up all on her own. Imagine getting pregnant — and having the baby! — right after you graduate high school. Would that mess up your life, or what?"

"Sure would," Peyton says. "Which reminds me, do you have condoms in that purse of yours, in case you get lucky with Rusty tonight?"

"Yes, Mom," Brooke says. "I'm all over the protection thing." She walks to the mirror and checks out her reflection. Adjusts a strap on the bustier, which peeks out flirtily from her tailored white Gap shirt. Then she whirls to face her friend. "I'm ready to rock! Let's go."

*   *   *

"Beautiful night, isn't it, darlin'?" Whitey Durham relaxes on the bench, looking like some sort of good ol' boy Buddha with his big tummy, his round head covered with a Orioles hat. He sighs. There's really no more peaceful place to be on a warm summer evening than right here, in Shady Hill Cemetery, talking to Camilla.

It's not like she talks back, but he's used to that. Camilla hasn't answered him for years now, not out loud, anyway. Frankly, he'd be a little taken aback if she did, since the dear woman is lying six feet under, beneath a beautifully carved granite stone reading CAMILLA DURHAM, BELOVED WIFE.

Whitey's a regular visitor. He comes when he's troubled, when he's happy, and when he just plain misses his sweetheart — which is pretty much all the time. Camilla meant the world to him, and she'll never be replaced.

She's a darn good listener, too.

"Guess I'll amble on down to the river in a little bit," Coach Durham goes on. "Remember how we used to watch the fireworks together? You were always holding your ears, saying the booms were too loud. But you sure did love the colors. 'Specially green. I remember that. You always did like green best."

"I like black myself," says a voice behind Whitey. "Raven black." Whitey jerks his head up and turns to see Dan Scott standing behind him.

"Dan," Whitey says. It's obvious that he's not overjoyed to see the man. First of all, he hates being interrupted when he's chatting with Camilla. And second, he hasn't had much use for Dan Scott for, oh, almost eighteen years now. Not since Whitey was coaching Dan as the star forward on that long-ago Ravens team. Or, rather, not since Dan walked out of Tree Hill, leaving a pregnant Karen behind. Sure, Whitey was the one who encouraged Dan to chase his dreams and grab the college scholarship he'd been offered. But once there was a baby in the picture, that plan should have changed. Whitey's always been a little shocked at the way Dan completely abandoned Karen and his son. Not that he should have been. Dan the boy was an arrogant, scheming, self-centered kid. Dan the man is just that same kid, all grown up.

"Whitey," Dan says, sitting down beside his old coach. "How's it hangin'?"

Whitey resents that kind of talk in front of Camilla. Graveyards are a place for respect and dignity. "I'm fine, Dan. How are you?" he answers a little stiffly.

"Can't complain," Dan says. "Business is great."

Whitey knows that Dan has sought him out for a reason. "What's up?" he asks, wondering what the man could possibly want from him, knowing it must have something to do with the prodigy.

Nathan.

Or, as Whitey sometimes thinks of him, "Dan, the Sequel."

Nathan's not a bad kid, but he does share some of his father's traits. And not just the good ones, like his incredible agility and grace on the basketball court. He also shares that whole egotistical "I'm the Star" attitude. Like he's the sun and the rest of his teammates are the planets. He wants to be the one calling the plays, planning the strategy. Whitey hasn't had an easy time convincing Nathan that one coach is enough, and that Whitey's name is on the payroll for that job. He never convinced Dan, all those years ago, either.

"It's about Nathan," Dan says, predictably. "I just want you to know that he's pouring his heart into keeping on top of his game this summer. He'll be carrying the team again this season, no doubt about it."

"Good to hear," Whitey says, uncertain as to what, exactly, Dan wants from him.

"What I'm saying is, you're gonna need to stay out of his way," Dan goes on. "Let him do what he knows how to do. Let him show off his stuff for the scouts." He pauses, but not long enough to let Whitey speak. "Nathan can go the distance," he says, almost under his breath. "He can do what I never got a chance to do."

Whitey is having a hard time believing what he's hearing. Dan's not asking, he's ordering — his bullying tone far beyond what Whitey would have believed him capable of. He could blow his top, shout at Dan that he's the coach, that he knows what he's doing, that the Ravens are a team, dammit, not just a vehicle for Nathan's stellar future. But he doesn't want to do that in front of Camilla. She always hated it when he yelled.

"Right," he says mildly instead, as if humoring a mental patient. "Got it." He stands up, dusts off his hands. "It's been —" He can't quite bring himself to say "a pleasure," so he just mumbles something.

Dan nods. "Happy Fourth of July, Whitey," he says.

"Same to you," Whitey answers. He blows a kiss to Camilla and plods away, toward the old green Ford parked at the cemetery gates.

Dan watches him go. *The guy is getting on*, he thinks. There was a time — wasn't there? — when Dan looked up to Whitey. Now he pretty much just thinks the coach is a stubborn old fool.

Dan gets off the bench, stretches, and jogs back to his car. He starts it up and takes off, driving aimlessly through town. Somehow, without quite meaning to, he ends up down by those junky old basketball courts down by the river. Easing into a spot that's hidden behind a thicket of gnarled cedars, he sits, car idling and air-conditioning blasting, and watches Karen's son play ball.

Dan's not hidden quite as well as he thinks he is. Out on the court, Lucas can't help being aware of the big shiny silver Lexus with dealer plates parked behind the trees. He knows exactly who's behind the wheel. He plays hard, driving to the basket over and over, not letting up even when Junk pleads with him to take it easy.

"C'mon, dude," Junk says. "It's, like, a hundred percent humidity out here. How about a break?"

Lucas pulls up his shirt to wipe sweat from his face. "I'll give you a break," he says teasingly. He fakes left, right, left again. "Fast break!" he says, bulling his way toward the hoop one more time.

He grins at his teammate Skills. Skills doesn't grin back. Skills hasn't been grinning much at all lately, Lucas realizes. But there's no time to wonder why. He's got the ball again, and he shoots from outside the paint to sink a gorgeous, deep three-pointer.

He doesn't want to look over at the Lexus, but he can't help himself. He glances over, wondering what the driver of that car — his father — is thinking. Did he see the shot? Did he think it was good? Does Lucas's playing remind him of his own game, when he was Lucas's age?

Lucas shakes the thoughts out of his mind. Why is he even spending one millisecond of his time on that jerk? He turns to pass the ball to Skills, and the next time he gets a chance to look, the Lexus has disappeared.

Good.

Lucas and Skills win, 15–12. After a brief postgame interview with Mouth, the guys sit drinking Gatorade and cooling down. There isn't even a puff of a breeze off the river today, and the air feels thick enough to float on.

Mouth and Edwards are still arguing over stats — should Skills get an assist for that layup? — and Junk and Fergie are talking about which girls they plan to hit on during the festivities that night. Lucas and Skills are off to one side, not saying much at all.

Lucas is brooding about Dan's appearance at the court, and Skills is just plain quiet. Lucas turns to him. "What's up, man?" he asks. "Everything okay?" He knows that Skills and his stepdad, Richie, don't always get along, especially when Richie is drinking. Maybe they're arguing again.

Skills just shrugs. "It is what it is," he says in a monotone.

Lucas gets the message. Skills doesn't want to talk about it.

"Okay, bro," he says, grabbing his towel and hopping off the picnic table. "See you later, then?" He holds out a fist and Skills gives him a pound. Lucas wants to say something about how Skills can always come to him if he wants to talk — but he doesn't want to sound girly. He hopes the fist-pound gets the message across.

It hasn't cooled down much by the time everyone starts drifting down to the river for Tree Hill's big Fourth of July bash. Lucas and Haley decide to walk, even though Karen and Keith offer them a ride in

Keith's wrecker. "I need to get that hot-dog smell out of my nose," Haley explains. Even though she's taken a shower and changed clothes, the Dog Kart aroma still clings. Lucas insists he doesn't smell it, but Haley knows he's lying.

"Okay, then," says Keith, helping Karen into the body shop's truck. He's happy to have her to himself. When Lucas is around, Karen is totally focused on her son. He's been the center of her life for so long; even now that he's almost grown the connection is still her first priority.

"Why, thank you," Karen says as Keith gently closes the truck door behind her. Her eyes are twinkling and the corner of her mouth lifts. She's a little amused by this sudden gentlemanly behavior.

Keith gets in on the driver's side and slams his own door — twice. The catch has been sticky for a while. Then he turns to smile at Karen. "I know, I know," he says. "It's not a date. I get that. But I can still treat you nice, can't I?"

It's odd how close they are, he sometimes thinks. He and Karen got to know each other when she and Dan started going out during high school, and he always thought the world of her. Secretly, he always thought he'd make a better boyfriend than Dan — and his opinion on that matter sure didn't change when Dan ditched Karen when she was pregnant.

Keith did his best to make up for his brother's crappy behavior in the following months. He took Karen to doctor's appointments, helped her find an apartment when her parents kicked her out, fixed up a room for a nursery, even offered to be with her when she gave birth. She passed on that one, but he did get to see Lucas when the little guy was only two hours old, and he'll never forget that moment. When he and the tiny, squalling baby looked at each other, he felt an immediate bond. The wave of emotion was so strong that it brought tears to his eyes. Since that moment, he's always felt superprotective of Lucas. He knows he's not the boy's dad, but he doesn't see what's wrong with being the best damn uncle he can be.

'Course, he wouldn't mind being the boy's dad, or rather his stepdad. But Karen's never given him any sign that she considers him anything other than a very good friend. So he mostly keeps his feelings to himself and just tries to enjoy any time he and Karen get to share.

Like tonight. They'll have a grand time down at the fireworks. Maybe she'll even go on the Ferris wheel with him. He smiles again, this time to himself. There's something about being with Karen on this warm summer night: It makes him feel like a kid again.

His smile fades as he pulls up to a stoplight next to a silver Lexus with dealer plates.

Dan sits gripping the wheel, staring straight ahead and pretending not to see the hulking tow truck that has just pulled up next to him.

"Oh, get over yourself!" cries his wife, Deb, when she notices Dan acting like he doesn't notice Keith and Karen. "He's your brother, for Pete's sake. When are you going to stop avoiding him and Karen?"

"When are you going to stop avoiding your own family?" he fires back. He knows it's lame, but he resents it when Deb steps back into his life and pretends to know anything about it. "You've been away on business for six weeks out of the last eight. Don't you think Nathan misses having his mom around?"

"I miss him, too," she says. "And I miss you, Dan, though I don't know why. Seems like when I'm home, all we do is bicker." She sighs. "I know I've been putting a lot of energy into my career lately. It won't always be this way, I promise. Just bear with me, can't you?"

Dan shrugs. "I try," he says. "But mac-and-cheese out of a box and takeout pizza are getting pretty old."

"Is that the only reason you miss having me around? No home-cooked meals?" Deb tries to keep her tone light, but the hurt in her voice is obvious. "May I remind you that I did the mom thing for twelve years solid, while you built up your business? And that I never got to finish college, since I — we — got pregnant before Thanksgiving of our freshman year?"

Dan sighs. He's heard this song before, and the

tune is getting old. He knows she's right, but he just doesn't have it in him to be Mr. Supportive Husband. He wants a wife, a companion, somebody who'll be there to talk to when he comes home from a long day. Plus, Nathan really does miss her. Dan's fine with parenting when it comes to the discipline part, but he has to admit he doesn't always do that nurturing thing so well. Nathan needs a mom.

So maybe it's better to keep the peace, encourage Deb to stick around for a while. He reaches over, puts a hand on hers. "I know, babe," he says. "You're doing what you need to do, and you're doing great. Nathan and I are really proud of you. We just miss you, that's all. And" — he shoots her his sweetest forgive-me grin — "not just for the home-cooked meals."

At the moment, Nathan doesn't seem to be missing his mom at all. He's strutting along with Peyton on one arm and Brooke on the other, feeling like a million bucks. Other guys are glancing at him enviously, and why not? He's with the two prettiest, sexiest chicks in a fifty-mile radius. Granted, Brooke's a bit of a basket case, and Peyton's ticked off at him for something (what else is new?), but nobody else has to know that. As far as the public knows, Nathan's taking both hotties home with him tonight for a game of naked Twister.

Tree Hill's downtown riverfront park has been transformed into a carnival, complete with rides, a midway full of shooting galleries and other games, and stands selling every variety of fried food on the planet. The smell of splattering grease mixes with the aroma of old, spilled beer emanating from the beer tent and the fragrance of diesel from the generators running the Tilt-A-Whirl, the Ferris wheel, and the dreaded Pirate Ship, on which Nathan hurled monumentally when he was in second grade. There's the sound of shrieks from the rides, cheesy music from the grandstand where some lousy local country band is playing, and fake gunfire from the shooting gallery games.

"Hey, dude, you look like a sharpshooter," calls

out the carny running one of them, gesturing at Nathan. "Hit three ducks with ten shots and win your girlfriend a biker bear." He holds up a bear dressed in a motorcycle outfit. "I'll make that two bears," he adds, "since you got both hands full tonight." He grins leeringly at Brooke, displaying a few missing teeth. She rolls her eyes and pulls her shirt closed over her bustier.

"Want a bear?" Nathan asks Peyton.

She shakes her head. "I wanted to see the parade," she says, pouting a little. "We missed it because you just had to finish that stupid game with Tim." When she and Brooke arrived to pick up Nathan, he was involved in a major PlayStation duel with his buddy. He made Brooke and Peyton wait while they finished.

"Told you I was sorry," Nathan says.

"I'm over it," says Peyton, who's obviously not. She has this weird thing about parades: She loves them. There's something about the sound of a marching band, the big bass drum and all.

"Who cares about the stupid parade?" Brooke asks happily. "Look around. Everybody's here." She takes another sip of her Coke, which she laced liberally with rum back in Peyton's car. It's her third drink, and she's clearly feeling no pain. "Including Doggie Girl and Nathan's bastard brother," she adds, giggling a little. She points to where Lucas and Haley are standing in line for the Ferris wheel. Nathan winces as Brooke starts to sing "Who Let the Dogs Out" at the top of her lungs. Lucas glares over at them, but Haley either doesn't hear or is very good at pretending she doesn't hear.

Then suddenly, Brooke stops singing. She grabs Peyton's arm. "Ohh," she sighs. "Crush alert!"

Peyton follows her friend's gaze and spots Rusty over by the Whack-A-Mole game, laughing with some friends — a pair of preppies in Dockers and polo shirts. Peyton has to admit that, at least next to those losers, Rusty looks pretty good in his black muscle tee and faded, ripped jeans. He may be a poseur, but hey, at least he's not wearing Dockers.

Peyton can feel Brooke drifting away, following the magnetic pull of her crush. "Go for it, babe," she says, giving Brooke a little pat on the behind as her friend takes off for the Whack-A-Mole.

Lucas and Haley sit at the very top of the Ferris wheel, looking out over their town. "I love how the lights of the McMansions on the Hill twinkle, just like our own little Milky Way," Haley says sarcastically.

"I love how the river shines in the moonlight," Lucas answers, meaning it. It hasn't always been easy growing up on the wrong side of the tracks in a town where everybody knows his business — but he loves his hometown just the same. He looks over at Haley. "You still smell like hot dogs," he says, laughing a little.

She scowls. "Have I mentioned how much I detest that job?" she asks.

"No, really?" Lucas asks. "You aren't happy there?" He gives her a poke. "It's only for the summer," he says. "You'll survive."

"Maybe." Haley isn't so sure. "Hey, isn't that Skills down there?" She points to a figure threading its way through the crowd. "What's he carrying?"

"Looks like a duffel bag," Lucas says. "Yo, Skills!" he yells, cupping his hands around his mouth. Skills doesn't look up. Lucas has to wait until the Ferris wheel completes its lazy ride. Then he and Haley run through the crowd, trying to catch up with his friend.

"Skills!" Lucas says, tapping him on the shoulder when they spot him slouched near a fried-dough stand.

Skills turns.

"Oh, my god," says Haley, drawing in a breath.

Skills's lip is swollen and bruised. He has a black eye and another bruise on his cheek.

"Richie?" Lucas asks. Skills's stepfather definitely has some anger management issues. Lucas has had a feeling that things might be heating up over at Skills's house.

Skills nods. "He called me a lazy slacker one too many times. I guess I called him some names, too. Anyway, I'm outta there." He gestures to his duffel bag.

Lucas and Haley both know Skills is anything but a slacker. He works two jobs and helps take care of his younger sisters.

"But where are you going?" Haley asks. She's not crazy about her family, but she can't imagine heading out on her own. Not for a couple years, anyway.

Skills shrugs. "Shelter?" he asks.

"Wrong," Lucas says, reaching over to pick up the duffel. "Let's go find my mom. You're staying with us."

The fireworks are reaching a crescendo, filling the sky with huge bursts of gold, green, and blue. The air reverberates with thunderous booms, and Peyton slips an arm around Nathan's waist. Laying her head on his shoulder, she sighs. He gives her a squeeze.

"I'm a little worried about Brooke," Peyton whispers as another rocket whistles its way up and bursts above them, showering silver sparkles in an enormous umbrella shape over their heads. Brooke and Rusty haven't been anywhere in sight since the sky darkened and the fireworks began.

Nathan gives her another squeeze. "That girl can

take care of herself," he assures Peyton. He glances over at his mom and dad, who also have their arms around each other. Deb's face is tilted up; she's watching the fireworks. But Dan is looking over at a group of people standing in the shadow of the Tilt-A-Whirl ticket booth. Nathan squints . . . and sees that his father is keeping a close eye on Lucas and Karen. Maybe Dan is a little worried about someone, too.

July 30

What I'm listening to today: The Doors,
"When You're Strange"

"Faces come out of the rain...when
you're strange."
      Am I strange?
      Possibly.
      Probably.
      But maybe I'm not really any
stranger than anyone else. Maybe
I'm just -- more aware of my own
strangeness. Like, why am I so afraid
to let my boyfriend know who I really
am? If he doesn't love the me I like
best, then maybe he's not The One.
      Maybe that's what I'm afraid
of....

    entry, Peyton's blog

Peyton stares at her computer screen. Does she really want to post this entry? She actually has no idea who reads her blog, if anyone. It's a pretty good bet that Nathan wouldn't bother, but you never know. People can surprise you.

What if he does read it? He must know that she has doubts. He probably has plenty of his own. She's crazy about him, but she doesn't kid herself. They're not soul mates, never will be.

But something Brooke said to her has been stuck in her mind. It was a couple of weeks ago, one day when Brooke was over. A rare visit, now that she's constantly hanging out on campus, specifically in Rusty's dorm room. Anyway, Brooke was checking out a drawing Peyton has had posted on her wall for the last couple months. It's just a little doodle really. An alien with a big head and gigantic eyes. "This is so cool," said Brooke. "I bet Nathan likes it."

"Nathan?" Peyton was surprised. "Nathan hasn't seen it."

"Oh, come on," Brooke said. "Don't bother pretending that he hasn't been in your room."

"I wasn't!" Peyton said. "He's here all the time. He just — never looks at my work, that's all."

"Too busy looking at you," Brooke said, smiling. "Or . . . just too busy, period," she added with a wink.

Peyton glanced at the bed, thinking about the hours Nathan and she have spent there. "Hmmm, maybe," she said. "Anyway, he just doesn't seem to notice my sketches. I don't think he even realizes they're my work."

Now it was Brooke's turn to say, "Hmm." She gave Peyton a serious look. "He's missing out if he doesn't know what an awesome artist you are. I mean, isn't that, like, a pretty big part of you for him not to know about?"

"I guess," said Peyton. "So, how's Rusty?" she asked. She knows how to make Brooke drop the subject. Sure enough, for the next fifteen minutes, all she was required to say was "Wow!" and "Really?" while Brooke chattered away happily.

Now Peyton glances up at the alien drawing again. She has the uncomfortable feeling that Brooke was right on. Before, it didn't bother her that Nathan never noticed her artwork. But now she can't stop thinking about it. So she's made a decision.

She looks down at the sketchpad next to her keyboard. She's been working for days on a sketch of Nathan. It's from a picture she cut out of the sports pages near the end of last season, a shot of him looking as if he's hanging in air as he drops in a jump shot. Brooke remembers the game; it was one of the Ravens' closer ones. Nathan scored a ton of points. That was before they were going out, but after Peyton had begun to think he was kind of cute, after all.

Anyway, here's what she's decided: When the sketch is finished, she's going to give it to Nathan. Yup, she's going to come out of the closet and let him know her deepest, darkest secret: She's an artist. Or, at least, a wannabe.

And it better be finished soon. Like — Peyton looks up to check the time on her computer's tool-bar — in four hours. She's decided to give it to him tonight at the party.

The party.

This will probably be THE party of the summer. Nobody's talked about anything else for weeks. It's going to be at the Scotts' house, and it's going to be huge. Peyton has heard that kids from as far away as Springfield have been talking about it. Lucky thing is, they don't really have to keep it a secret: Nathan's dad already knows all about it. In fact, it was kind of his idea. A reward, Nathan told Peyton, for all the work he's been doing to keep in shape and train for basketball season.

Dan believes that it's good for kids — boys especially, Peyton bets — to "blow off steam" once in a while. Peyton's not so sure that Nathan's mom agrees with this theory, but she's in Chicago on business and doesn't have a clue.

Peyton adds a little more shading to Nathan's jaw, thinking as she does it that while she's not overly revved about the party itself, she is psyched to give him this picture. It'll be, like, a step forward in their relationship. And she wants to go deeper with Nathan — doesn't she?

*   *   *

"Hold on a sec," Haley says to Lucas. She turns away from him and hollers to her boss. "Yo! Pete! We're almost out of fries," she yells. Then she turns back, all smiles. "I'm kinda getting into the rhythm of this place," she admits.

"Getting used to the hat, too?" Lucas asks.

Haley makes a face. "Never." She reaches up to adjust the dachshund on her head. "Never, never, never."

Lucas grins. "So, Hales, whattaya say about tonight?"

"I say the same thing I've been saying all week," Haley says. "Never, never, never."

"Come on," Lucas pleads. "I would do it for you!"

"Would you? Maybe. But we'll never find out," Haley says, "because I'd never ask you to." She reaches over the counter to grab his hand. "We don't belong there," she says, looking into his eyes. "River rats at a Hill party? Uninvited rats? We're just asking to be humiliated. I don't even understand why you'd want to go."

Lucas has been trying to convince Haley to go to Nathan's party. Not that they were invited or anything. Like there's a chance that would ever happen. But he's heard the buzz. He knows that there'll be a huge crowd there and figures that one or two more won't matter. And lately, he's just been kind of — curious — about what it would be like to be in Nathan's world. He doesn't want to live there, but he'd kind of like to visit. Not without his best friend, though.

"Come on," he pleads again. "I'll buy you a" — he looks around desperately — "a SuperDeluxe Mega-Dog," he says, spotting the most expensive item on the menu.

Haley pretends to stick a finger down her throat. "No sale," she tells Lucas. "Sorry, bud."

Lucas tries to think of a better bribe, but just then he hears a throbbing bass and a wailing guitar behind him. He recognizes the song: It's the Clash, "London Calling." He turns to see the Comet pulling into the parking lot, Peyton behind the wheel. "Ah," he mutters to Haley as they watch Peyton, Brooke, and Nathan climb out of the car and saunter toward the Kart. "It's the Thrilling Threesome." He steps aside as they approach, ignoring Nathan as studiously as Nathan ignores him.

Haley pastes on a smile. "What can I get you?" she asks, grateful that Brooke doesn't seem to be half-wrecked on hard lemonade this time. Maybe she'll be spared the serenade.

Nathan orders enough food for three people. Then he turns to Peyton and Brooke. "You guys want something, too?"

Haley hides a smile while Brooke and Peyton debate, finally agreeing to split an order of onion rings. Haley gets their food and they go off to the picnic table to eat it.

Lucas comes back to the window to chat some more with Haley, each of them keeping half an eye on the action at the picnic table. "How's Skills doing?" Haley asks.

"Better," says Lucas. "He's definitely happy to be out of Richie's way. And he sure does like Mom's cooking."

"He should," Haley says. "Karen is the best cook in town."

"I know," Lucas says. "I wish everybody else knew, too. Maybe the cafe would actually pay our bills."

Karen is the owner and cook at Karen's Cafe, a small, homey place housed in what used to be a bookstore. She serves up breakfast in the morning, great sandwiches for lunch, and soup, chili, and pie for dinner. She has some loyal customers — some people hang out for hours, lounging in the over-stuffed easy chairs and reading or working on their laptops — but the place hasn't exactly taken off. Lucas knows that she went pretty far into debt to get the place up and running, and it's going to be a long time before it pays itself off — if that ever happens. Still, owning a cafe was a dream of Karen's, and even though she works her butt off, she's happy.

Lucas glances over at Nathan. What would it be like to be rich? To never have to worry about the elec-tricity being turned off because you couldn't pay the bills? To feel like the world is yours, and you can do whatever you want? He can't really even imagine it, but he wants it. Not for himself — he's fine with things the way they are. But his mom deserves better.

Lucas is working himself up into an old, familiar anger toward Dan Scott and the way he abandoned Karen when Haley cocks a head toward the picnic table. "What do you think they're giggling about?" she whispers.

Lucas looks over. Peyton seems bored and ready to leave, but Brooke and Nathan have their heads together as if they're hatching some plan. "I double-dare you," he hears Brooke say. "No, I triple-dare you."

Nathan stands up and saunters over to the window, leaving his tray and all the trash from his gargantuan meal on the table. He looks straight at Lucas and gives one of those little "hey, dude" nods. "So," he says, turning to include Haley, "I'm, like, having this party tonight. You guys should come if you can." He turns and leaves before Lucas or Haley can say a word. Peyton has started up the Comet, and with a blast of screaming guitars, they're off.

Haley stares after them, openmouthed. "What was that all about?"

Lucas shrugs. "They're just messing with us."

"But we're invited!" Haley seems to have taken the invitation seriously.

"Yeah — like, on a dare," Lucas says.

"I don't care," Haley says. "If we're invited, we're going."

Lucas can't believe what he's hearing. "What? Now you're all, like, let's go to the ridiculous Hill people party?"

"Uh-huh," Haley says happily. "I get off at six. Pick me up at eight." Then she turns to a customer who has been waiting patiently at the window. "And what can I get you, ma'am?" she asks, without another glance at Lucas.

Lucas picks Haley up at eight, as ordered. "Wow, you look awesome," he says when she climbs into the wrecker he's borrowed from Keith. She does, too. She's just wearing jeans and a tank top, but there's something different about her hair — it's all shiny, and it smells good — and he thinks she's wearing some makeup.

"What, I'm gonna go to Nathan Scott's beach house in my Dog Kart uni?" she asks. "I'm representing my people here. I want these guys to know that river girls can be just as hot as those Hill chicks."

Lucas raises his eyebrows. Haley never ceases to surprise him.

"You look nice, too," she says. "I bet Peyton's gonna be checking you out."

"Peyton?" Lucas asks. "Nathan's girlfriend? What are you talking about?" And why is his heart thudding in his chest?

"She looks at you," Haley says. "I notice these things."

Lucas decides to change the subject. "I guess we're here," he says, trying to find a place to put the truck. There are already about twenty cars parked up and down the tree-lined street.

Haley looks around. "I've never even been in this neighborhood before," she says. "How much do you think these places cost?" The street only has about five houses on it, each of them huge and set well back from the road, with wide, rolling lawns and tasteful shrubbery. Each house looks big enough for three families.

It's not hard to spot the Scott house. It's the one with all the lights on. The doors are open, and people and music spill out into the gathering dusk.

"You ready for this?" Lucas asks.

"Ready as I'll ever be," says Haley, taking a deep breath. "Let's go."

By midnight, the party is pretty much out of control — and Nathan is loving it. He cruises through the house, taking in the scene. Most of his buddies from the team are in the backyard, hanging around the keg and watching the action at the pool, where some girls are threatening to go skinny-dipping. There are stoners doing bong hits in the basement rec room, half-naked couples making out in the living room, and a major rave going on in the great room, the one with the huge fireplace and high ceiling. The music is so loud in there he can feel it in his bones, and people are crushed up against one another, moving like one solid mass. Nathan doesn't even recognize at least a third of the people in there.

He's spotted Lucas a couple of times: The loser actually took his invitation seriously and showed up with that Dog Kart girl. Nathan's also spotted that bro who showed up at the Fourth of July looking seriously messed up, like he'd just gone a few rounds in the boxing ring. He's hanging out with Lucas and the girl, none of them looking all that comfortable.

There's also broken glass on the front steps, a red wine stain on his mom's favorite rug, an overflowing toilet on the second floor, and evidence of someone blowing major chunks in one of the flowerpots on the patio.

It's a party. No doubt about it.

"Hey, man," he says to a guy he sort of recognizes. The guy nods, but keeps walking in a determined way, heading for the keg. Then Nathan sees Brooke's red-haired college-dude boyfriend, and remembers that the first guy is one of Rusty's preppy pals. He's a little surprised that a bunch of college guys would come to the party, but then again he knows that Brooke can be pretty persuasive.

"Hey, babe," he says, spotting Peyton coming through with Brooke and Rusty. "'Sup," he says to Rusty. He throws an arm around Peyton. "Having fun?" he asks. She's looking hot tonight, with her hair all tousled and wild. He wonders if she's planning to hang out after everybody else leaves.

"Hey," she says, "I have something for you." Peyton realizes that it's now or never: She'd better give Nathan the sketch before he gets any drunker if she wants him to really see it.

"What? Is it in here?" Nathan pulls out the top of her shirt and tries to look down it.

Peyton slaps his hand away. Maybe he's already too wrecked.

"What?" Nathan asks, all innocent. "It's not like I haven't seen 'em before."

Peyton just gives him a look.

"Sorry, sorry," he says. "So, what is it really?"

Peyton goes over to a pile of stuff she left near the door, opens up her sketchbook, and pulls out the picture. She takes one last look at it. It's pretty good. Not the best thing she ever drew, but she likes it. She carries it back over to Nathan and puts it in his hands. "This is for you," she says, trying to sound casual. "I drew it."

Nathan looks at the sketch. "Hey! Check it out!" he says. "Is that, like, supposed to be me?"

Peyton nods. Her face feels hot.

"Hey, Tim, look at this!" He grabs a teammate who's walking by. "Peyton drew it."

"Awesome," Tim says after a glance.

A bunch of people start gathering around Nathan, looking over his shoulder at the picture and commenting on it. Even Lucas and Haley join the crowd, craning their necks for a look at the sketch. Brooke gives Peyton's shoulder a squeeze. "See?" she whispers. "He thinks you're even cooler now."

Then Nathan ruins it all. He starts to laugh. "I don't believe this," he says. "Look at the way she drew my arms. They look like sticks! I wouldn't be bench-pressing one-fifty if I really had arms like that." He keeps laughing. "And what's up with the nose? What am I, Pinocchio?"

Peyton's face turns bright red. She steps forward and snatches the sketch out of Nathan's hands. Then she whirls around and stalks out of the room.

"Oops," says Nathan.

Brooke sneers at him. "Yeah," she says. "Oops." She goes after her friend, working her way through a maze of hallways. But when she spots Peyton, she puts on the brakes. Standing right next to her is Lucas!

"Who's that?" Rusty asks. He's followed Brooke down the hall.

Brooke looks at him. "It's Nathan's brother," she says. "Sort of. It's complicated."

"What, you think I'm too dumb to get it?" Rusty asks, his voice rising a bit.

"I didn't say that," Brooke says.

"You meant it, though," Rusty says. Now his voice

is definitely loud, verging on shouting. He's had at least six beers, and now Brooke remembers that he was doing tequila shots in the kitchen, too.

"No, no," she says. "C'mon, babe, I was just –" She puts a hand on his chest.

He brushes it away. "Did I ask you to touch me?" he bellows. "Don't treat me like a moron, and don't touch me unless I tell you to. Follow those rules, and you can be my bitch. Otherwise, there's plenty in line to take your place."

By now, Lucas and Peyton are staring at Brooke and Rusty. Plus, Nathan and his buddies have crammed themselves into the hallway. A bunch of other people are peering over their shoulders. It's like the whole party is suddenly in this one, tight spot.

Now Brooke's face is on fire. She's used to Rusty talking to her this way; he's been doing it more and more. Usually he's really sweet afterward, and they have a lot of fun making up. But it's different when he does it in front of other people. In front of her friends.

Lucas takes a step away from Peyton, toward Rusty. "Hey," he says. "Maybe it's getting late. Maybe it's time for people to start heading home . . . or wherever," he adds, spotting Skills in back of Nathan.

"Oh, so now you're, like, a diplomat?" Nathan says. There is something really unsettling about seeing that guy Lucas next to Peyton. He's probably all sensitive and romantic, the kind of guy chicks dig. Nathan isn't even sure exactly why Peyton's so upset with him, but he senses that he did something to make her mad — and that this Lucas dude was, like, comforting her. "This is my house, and my party, and I'll tell people when it's time to leave," he says, folding his arms. "And I'm telling you to take off now. House rule: No bastards after midnight."

He hears the gasps all around him. Oh, yeah. People are going to be talking about this party for a while. Nathan grins — and then collapses to the floor as Skills tackles him from behind.

The place erupts.

Within seconds, there's a full-scale brawl going on. It spills out of the hallway into the house, and out of the house and onto the lawn. Nathan's teammates are banging away on Lucas and Skills. Peyton, Brooke, and Haley are screaming, trying to pull people apart. Rusty and his friends jump in just for fun, throwing fists and yelling as they wrestle whoever's closest. The whole party empties out to watch, yelling encouragement and advice.

"What the hell?"

Dan can't believe his eyes. He told Nathan he'd be checking in around midnight and that he expected things to be under control. That was part of their deal. This is not what he would call "under control." He can hear some kind of brawl going on inside. And as he comes up the walk he sees a light come on in the house next door. Tree Hill's finest are probably going to show up any minute. Deb is never going to let him forget it if the party gets busted.

Dan flips open his cell phone, punches in a number. "Get over here quick," he says into the phone. "Call Whitey, too."

Minutes later, Keith Scott pulls up in his car, Whitey next to him in the front seat. Both men jump out.

It's obvious that Whitey has dealt with this kind of thing before. He swings right into action. "Dan, go get rid of any alcohol in the house or out by the pool," he directs. "Keith, shut down that hellacious noise they're dancing to." Whitey strides up to Nathan, who's quickly disentangled himself from the scuffle at the sight of his father. "Son, do me a favor. Find two or three of your friends who aren't wrecked out of their minds. Round up everybody's car keys, and we'll organize some carpools to get these poor slobs home."

By the time Officer Jenkins pulls up in his cruiser, things are looking much better. Dan sits on the stoop next to Keith, sighing with relief as he watches Whitey head up the walk to talk to the police. He may not get along all that well with his former coach or his big brother, but he knows who he can count on in a crisis.

August 15

"May your trails be crooked, winding,
lonesome, dangerous, leading to the most
amazing view. May your mountains rise into
and above the clouds." – Edward Abbey,
naturalist and author (1927-1989)

I came across this quote yesterday and
had to add it to my collection. I like how
Abbey is saying, "Sure, life is difficult. But
that's part of what makes it so incredible."
You can't shy away from the hard stuff. In
fact, maybe the thing to do is to embrace it,
the way Abbey urges us to do. Yeah. That's
easy to say, but

unfinished entry, Lucas's journal

Lucas hears footsteps in the hall. Skills must be
back from his early-morning run. The guy just never
sits still. If he's not at one of his jobs, or working out,

he's helping Karen in the kitchen or fixing the leak in the bathroom sink. Lucas shakes his head. Whatever makes his friend happy is fine with him. And Skills does seem a lot happier since he left home. He and his mom and stepdad have started some family therapy sessions, but Lucas isn't convinced that Skills will ever live in that house again.

The footsteps come closer. Lucas tucks his journal between his mattress and box spring. It's not that he doesn't trust Skills — it's just that his journal is the one place where he lets it all hang out. He'll write anything in there, knowing that his eyes will be the only ones to see it. Mostly, though, it's just a collection of cool quotations he finds. Like the one he wrote down a few days ago. Something Albert Einstein once said: "Life is like riding a bicycle. To keep your balance you must keep moving." Lucas loves that. Somehow stuff like that just gets to him.

"Hey, dude," Skills says, coming through the door. He flops onto the twin bed closer to the door, the one he's been sleeping on. Skills isn't a huge guy, but he kind of fills up the room. He pulls a knee to his chest, stretching.

"Good run?" Lucas asks.

Skills shrugs. "A run's a run," he says philosophically. "But yeah, it was okay. Looks like it's gonna be hot again."

"They'll have to scrape melting tourists off the sidewalk," Lucas says. Today is Tree Hill Is Terrific Day, a pseudo-holiday dreamed up by the Chamber of Commerce in an attempt to pump up the tourist traffic in town. Every year it gets a little more elaborate: First there was just an art show and craft fair. Then they added a food court, a music tent, and a bunch of activities like historical tours, a 5K running race, and a toy-boat regatta out on the river. The event goes on all day and into the evening.

The big new thing this year is "Tree Hill Is Talented," sort of an open mic night/talent show. The corny name makes Lucas wince, but he knows at least one band that's appearing and figures he'll check it out. Meanwhile, his main hope is to avoid interaction with tourists as much as possible. Last year he had to take the wrecker out onto High Street, negotiating a major traffic jam to haul off some dude's Beemer after he collided with a minivan. Just a fender bender, but what a headache.

Skills bounces back up off the bed, ready for the next thing. "Gonna be down at the court later?" he asks.

"Oh, yeah," Lucas says. "I'll be at the shop for a while. I'll head down after lunch."

"Catch you later, then," Skills says, throwing the peace sign.

"Later," Lucas echoes.

When the door closes, he gets up and goes over to the computer on his desk. It's a castoff from Keith's shop, all dinged and tired, but it works. Lucas is used to how slow the dial-up connection is; he'd better be, since Karen will never spring for DSL. He boots up, dials in, and checks his e-mail. Then he surfs over to Peyton's webcam and blog. He's not really sure why he goes there all the time. It's not like he's hoping to catch her naked or something — though it's not like he'd sign off if he did. It's just — she's not what he expected. Mainly what she does when she's in her room is listen to music and draw. She's good, too. She's posted some of her sketches, and Lucas is impressed. He's also impressed with her musical taste; a cheerleader who loves Hole, Neil Young, Blur, and the Dead Kennedys is definitely not your average cheerleader.

He rereads a blog entry that he finds especially interesting.

Am I strange? it says. *Possibly. But maybe I'm not really any stranger than anyone else. Maybe I'm just — more aware of my own strangeness. Like, why am I so afraid to let my boyfriend know who I really am? If he doesn't love the me I like best, then maybe he's not The One.*

Maybe that's what I'm afraid of. . . .

Lucas stares at the screen, wondering if Peyton has any idea how reading that makes him feel. Then he realizes that even he doesn't really know how it makes him feel. Weird, that's all. Strange, to use her word. Sometimes he wishes he could e-mail her anonymously and tell her she is definitely not strange. She's — cool.

Lucas checks his watch, realizes he's late for work, and signs off in a hurry. He heads downstairs to grab a piece of toast, then takes off for Keith's shop.

Haley scribbles in her notebook, frantically trying to get down the phrase that just popped into her mind. She never knows what images might make their way into one of her songs. A guy approaches the window, checking out the menu. Haley tries to get one more word down while he's deciding on his order.

"Hey, help the man!" Pete yells from behind the grill. "Shake it, kiddo. I'm not payin' you to take notes."

Haley snaps the notebook shut. "Can I help you, sir?" she asks, adjusting her Dog Kart hat so that the tail isn't tickling her neck.

"In a minute," he says, like she's bugging him.

Haley doesn't dare open the notebook again. Pete has been on her case since they opened. It's really getting her down, too. She has been fantasizing about quitting for days now.

She and Pete got along okay at first, but lately he's been cranky all the time, and he takes it out on her. Haley thinks maybe things aren't going so well for him at home; she's overheard more than a couple of nasty arguments between Pete and Dixie, his wife. She comes in all dressed to kill, teased-blond hair piled up high and spike heels tripping along. She always wants money for shopping. Pete never wants to give her any. They have the same fight every time. And when she leaves, Pete is always in a crappy mood.

"What?" he asks now, noticing that she's turned around, looking at him.

"Nothing," Haley says. Once again, she had been dreaming about the exact words she might use to let Pete know she'd be moving on. But she won't. She can't afford to. She really needs this job, and it's too late to find another for the summer. Everybody knows that school starts in a couple weeks; nobody's going to hire her now.

She glances back at Pete one more time. His greasy black hair and the blurry old tattoos on his hairy arms are really starting to gross her out. *So don't look*, she tells herself. She grabs a rag and starts to wipe down the counter before he can yell at her about slacking between customers.

As she wipes, she hums to herself. She's still working on that "Dog Days of Summer" song she started in June. She feels like it's almost there. "Workin' my way," she sings, swiping the rag up over the milk-shake mixer, "through the dog days of summer. . . ."

"Sounds like your theme song."

Haley stops in midnote and looks up to see Lucas smiling at her through the window. "Yeah," she says, smiling back.

"Never heard that one," Lucas says. "Lucinda?"

He knows she's a big Lucinda Williams fan. "Nope," she says. "On your way to the court?" She doesn't want any more questions. Writing and singing songs is Haley's secret pleasure, and she's shy about it — even around Lucas.

Lucas nods. "Where else?" He leans in to the window. "Maybe we'll head downtown later, check out the action?"

"Tree Hill Is Terrific!" Haley says with false enthusiasm. "Wish I could, but I can't. I'm working late tonight." She's bummed about that. She had been having this wild idea that she might enter the talent show, if she could find the courage.

"Yo, Tinkerbell," shouts Pete from behind her. "Think you might get around to some work sometime today?"

Haley brandishes her rag at him. "I'm working, I'm working," she says.

"Right," says Pete. "Workin' on your social life. Don't forget, you're on my dime now. You want to flirt with your boyfriend, do it on your own time."

"He's not —" Haley begins, starting to defend herself. Then she realizes she's wasting her time. Whether or not Lucas is her boyfriend isn't the point.

"You know," Lucas says to her, "you shouldn't have to put up with this kind of crap. You work hard here."

Haley bugs out her eyes at him. If he's not careful, Pete's going to overhear him, and she'll get canned.

Lucas ignores her. "I mean, employees deserve respect from their bosses, don't you think?"

Haley is still making faces at him. She doesn't realize that Pete has come right up behind her.

"You got a problem, pal?" Pete says threateningly. He pushes Haley aside and puts both hands on the counter, leaning into Lucas's face.

"Yeah, pal," Lucas answers. "I do. I don't like seeing you treat my friend like dirt."

"What are you gonna do about it?" Pete asks.

A panicky Haley is looking from Pete to Lucas and back again. "Lucas," she says. "It's okay. Never mind." She has a bad feeling in the pit of her stomach.

"It's not what I'm gonna do," Lucas says. "It's what she's gonna do. She's walking out of here, right now. And you're gonna have to find somebody else to bully."

"Lucas!" Haley says.

"Trust me," Lucas mutters.

"You can't walk out," Pete says. "This is going to be the busiest night of the summer!"

"Oh, well!" Lucas says lightly. He walks over to the door at the end of the Kart and pulls it open. "Come on, Hales. Ditch the doggy hat and let's get out of here."

Haley looks at Pete. She can practically see the steam coming out of his ears. He's only going to treat her worse now. The next couple of weeks will be pure misery, and her measly paycheck isn't worth it. She takes off the ridiculous hat and sets it on the counter. Then she unties her apron, takes it off, folds it, and places it carefully next to the hat.

She's about to leave them there on the counter, but then she remembers she paid for them. Hideous as they are, they're hers. She grabs them and stuffs them into her backpack.

Pete is just standing there, arms folded, glowering.

"Sorry, Pete," Haley says, even though she's not. She heads out the door without looking back.

"Whoo-hoo!" shouts Lucas as they sprint away from the Kart.

"You are nuts!" Haley shouts back. "I needed that job!"

Lucas shakes his head. "You needed it yesterday," he says. "Before Sherri quit."

"Sherri?" Haley wonders if Lucas has lost his mind. "Who's Sherri?"

"You remember Sherri," Lucas says. "She waitresses at my mom's cafe. Well, she did. Until yesterday. Now you do."

"How can you listen to this junk?" Brooke yells over the din in Peyton's room.

"Junk?" Peyton shouts back. "This is Patti Smith, one of the coolest women in history. You should be honored beyond belief that I'm playing my precious vinyl copy of 'Horses' for you."

"What?" Brooke screams.

Peyton strides over to the Marantz and, grudgingly, lowers the volume from ten to seven. "Better?" she asks.

" 'Better' would be if you put on some normal music, like Usher or something," Brooke says. "But yes, at least my eardrums aren't about to implode."

Peyton's bed is covered with a pile of clothes: skirts, jeans, tanks, and shorts. A lacy purple bra tops the heap. It's Brooke's, of course. She and Peyton have convened to plan outfits for that night.

"Rusty is acting all weird lately," she complains to Peyton. "Like, sometimes he's all over me and acts jealous if I even talk to another guy. But other times he's all distant. Sometimes when I call, his roommate says he's out — but I can tell he's lying." She picks up the bra. "Rusty needs to be reminded of how lucky he is," she says, lying back on the bed. "I want to look extra, extra hot tonight."

"So we're talking mega-hot?" Peyton asks. "Surface-of-the-sun hot?" She grins at her friend. "I don't know if Tree Hill can take it."

Brooke slingshots the bra at her. "Shut up," she says. "Shut up and help me decide what to wear." She holds up a tiny white tank. "This would look so cool if I had my navel pierced," she says.

Lucas is an outsider at Tree Hill High – but he's determined to play for their basketball team, the Ravens.

But his half brother, Nathan, thinks the team is his and his alone.

Nathan has everything Lucas lacks — stardom on the court, popularity in the halls, and the prettiest girl in school as his girlfriend.

But there's a connection between Lucas and Peyton that won't seem to go away.

Dan Scott is father to both Nathan and Lucas — but Nathan is the favorite son.

The one thing Lucas is sure of is his best friend, Haley James.

Peyton's best friend, Brooke, is attracted to Lucas, too.

The river court is Lucas's turf —
but Nathan shows up there to
issue a challenge.

Haley warns Lucas about getting mixed up with Nathan and his crowd.

Lucas wants to prove that he doesn't feel inferior to Nathan — especially in front of Peyton.

Showdown time: Nathan and Lucas face off on the court.

"What about that red tube top?" Peyton asks. "With the white mini."

"I said I wanted to look hot, not like a ho," Brooke says. "All I'd need to make that outfit complete would be some huge platforms and big hair."

"I bet Rusty would be into that," Peyton says.

"Please," says Brooke. "Rusty's a college guy, remember? His taste is more on the sophisticated side." She picks up a slinky pink tee and pulls it on.

"Yeah, he's sophisticated, all right," Peyton says. "Like when he yelled at you right in the middle of the lobby at the movies the other night?"

Brooke pulls off the tee. "What are you saying?" she asks Peyton.

"I just think he's kind of — mean to you sometimes," Peyton says carefully. "You don't deserve that."

"You don't understand," Brooke tells Peyton. "He's under a lot of pressure. He's taking this summer course to make up some credits, and if he fails he might have to drop out. His parents would kill him." She's standing in front of the mirror now, holding up a gauzy white peasant blouse to see how it looks with her skirt.

"Whatever," Peyton says. "Just — be careful, okay?" She pulls on a black tee with SEX PISTOLS scrawled on the back.

"I'm not the only one who should be careful," Brooke mutters, stepping out of her skirt and pulling on a pair of cutoffs.

"What's that supposed to mean?" Peyton asks sharply.

"Nothing," says Brooke. "I mean, you probably don't want to know."

"Brooke," Peyton says. There's a warning tone in her voice. "What?"

"It's about Nathan," Brooke says, sitting down on the bed.

Peyton feels her stomach flip. She and Nathan have been getting along really well lately. He's been so sweet ever since the fallout from his party. He's apologized about a million times for making fun of her drawing of him. Once he even asked to see some more of her sketches. That hasn't happened yet, since they're kind of *busy* whenever they're in her room, but at least he's interested.

Peyton gets up and turns the stereo down another notch. "What about Nathan?" she asks, her voice flat.

"I saw him downtown the other day," Brooke reports hesitantly. "In the courtyard by the post office." She stops.

"And?" Peyton prompts.

"And he was with a girl," Brooke finishes. "A red-head. I think she goes to Spaulding."

Spaulding is a school up north, one of Tree Hill's biggest sports rivals. "So? Nathan was talking to some girl," Peyton says.

"Not just talking," Brooke says. "Flirting. I can read body language a mile away, and the boy was definitely putting the moves on her."

Peyton decides she doesn't want to hear any more. She also decides that Brooke is just trying to get back at her for what she said about Rusty. She walks over to the Marantz and cranks it back up to ten. Then she starts sorting through the pile of clothes on the bed. Suddenly, she wants to look extra, extra hot that night, too.

"My hero," says Haley, overdoing the worshipping gaze as she mugs for Lucas. "I can't believe I'm never going to have to wear that heinous doggy hat again!"

"Wait till you see the new uniforms for waitresses at Karen's Cafe," says Karen. She and Keith and Haley and Lucas are squeezed into the front seat of the wrecker, on their way downtown for the evening's festivities.

Haley turns to look at her. "What?" she asks, her face frozen in fear. "You didn't tell me —"

"Kidding," says Karen quickly. "No uniform. Just make sure you're neat and clean and dressed decently. I don't want any of my regulars complaining about having to look at navel rings or tattoos."

"No worries," says Haley happily. She can't believe her luck. Not only is she out from under Pete's thumb, not only did Karen totally jump at the chance to hire her (for a job that will extend beyond summer, no less, and keep the money coming in through the school year, too), not only that, but since Karen decided to close the cafe for the night, Haley is free to do what she's been dreaming of: sing in the talent show.

Eek.

Haley gulps. Suddenly, the reality smacks her in the face. Is she really ready to stand on stage singing one of her own original compositions in front of a crowd that will include every soul she knows on the planet?

Not so much.

Don't be a wuss, she tells herself. *You can do it.*

But she's not so sure she can. Maybe she's not ready for an audience, or at least not an audience that huge. She looks over at Lucas and wonders if he would understand. He might. After all, as good as he is at playing basketball, he seems to prefer playing on that shabby little court with nobody but Mouth and Edwards for spectators.

Keith eases the truck into a parking spot two sizes too small, and they all pile out. Instead of being held down by the river, like the Fourth of July events, Tree Hill Is Terrific takes place right in the middle of downtown, on and around the big green. The streets are full of people, both locals and tourists. You can tell the tourists by the Tree Hill Is Terrific tees they're all wearing. There're lots of kids running around, too, holding free balloons given out by Bisbee's Toy Store. Haley looks past the food court, past the booths run by local groups like the Historical Society and the Raven Boosters Club, past the big tent where the craft show is taking place.

The only thing Haley's seeing is the big stage set up at one end of the green.

Eek.

She walks along with Lucas, Karen, and Keith, barely noticing where she's going or who she's passing. Until they pass the Raven Boosters booth, that is. Then she can't help but notice Dan Scott standing there, arms folded as he surveys the crowd. He's chatting with the blond woman who's running the booth, and both of them seem to recoil when they see Karen, Keith, and Lucas approaching.

"Hey, little brother," Keith says to Dan.

Dan nods but doesn't reply. He's working overtime to avoid looking Lucas in the eye.

Karen smiles at the blond woman.

The woman bares her teeth in return.

"Whoa," Haley says under her breath after they've passed by. "How awkward was that?"

Karen lets out a breath, half-laughter, half-sob. "It never gets easier seeing him," she admits.

Lucas is frowning, his eyes dark with anger. He glances back at the booth and catches Dan looking at him.

"Was that Mrs. Scott?" Haley asks.

Karen shakes her head. "Oh, no," she says. "Mrs. Scott is rarely around, as far as I know. Not that I blame her, given what she has waiting at home for her. No, that was — that was someone I used to know in high school."

"Was she a rhymes-with-witch then, too?" Haley asks.

Keith and Karen look at each other. "Oh, yeah," they chorus together.

That breaks the tension, and they all laugh.

Then Haley spots the stage again, and her smile fades.

If she's even considering singing, she has to go check the situation out. Fortunately, Mouth and Skills show up just then and start telling Lucas about a game he missed down at the court. Haley excuses herself and wanders off, working her way toward the stage.

At the other end of the green, Peyton and Brooke are sauntering along with Nathan and Rusty. There is no question, judging by the way guys are scoping them, that they have succeeded in their goal of looking extra, extra hot. Brooke is stunning in a blue halter top and short white shorts, Peyton is a knockout in a pink sundress.

Nathan has an arm slung around Peyton's shoulders, and he keeps whispering sweet things into her ear. He is looking at nobody but her, and she likes it that way.

Rusty keeps one hand in the back pocket of Brooke's shorts, like he's claiming ownership. She giggles whenever he gives her butt a little extra squeeze. So far, Peyton is relieved to see, he seems to be behaving decently.

"Let's grab some seats for the show," Peyton suggests. "The music should be starting soon."

"You're kidding," says Rusty. "We're really going to sit through a bunch of lame acts by untalented locals?"

Peyton bristles. "Who says they're untalented?" she asks. "I happen to know some of the musicians, and they're pretty good."

Rusty waves a hand. "Don't get all wack on me," he says. "I'll do whatever Bootsy here wants to do." He gives Brooke's shoulder a squeeze. Brooke smiles up at him.

Bootsy? Peyton feels like gagging, but she just smiles. "Great," she says. "You up for it, Nathan?"

"Whatever," he says, shrugging. Nathan never cares much what they do, as long as he gets his "back rub" at the end of the date. "I'm hungry, though."

"You find us some seats," Peyton says, "and I'll go grab some snacks. Deal?" Suddenly she's ready to head off by herself for a few minutes. She takes off without even waiting for an answer.

Threading her way through the crowd, Peyton spots a bunch of people she knows: other cheerleaders, Nathan's teammates, her advanced bio teacher — and Lucas. She seems to see him everywhere. Their eyes meet when they pass each other near a cotton-candy stand, but they don't exactly say hello. She would have expected him to be with that girl from the Dog Kart, but he's on his own at the moment, just like her. For a second, she considers stopping to talk to him. But — what would she say? "Hey, I'm out on a date with your brother" would be a heck of a conversation-stopper.

Peyton picks up some popcorn and sodas and, balancing it all carefully, starts working her way back to the concert area. When she finds herself in view of the stage, she starts looking around for Nathan, Brooke, and Rusty. She spots Brooke down near the front, on the right. Rusty's sitting next to her. But where's Nathan? Peyton starts toward the stage, scanning the crowd. She still doesn't see him. Then, just as she approaches Brooke and Rusty, she finally spots her boyfriend.

He's standing between two amps, having an intense conversation with a redheaded girl.

Peyton stares at him. She can't believe what she's seeing! She leaves the guy for five minutes, and what does he do?

Nathan doesn't see her. He leans closer to the girl, then actually reaches out and puts a hand on her shoulder as he laughs at something she's telling him.

Like Brooke said, there's no question about it. Body language never lies.

Peyton strides over, covering the ground in no time flat. Nathan glances up just in time to see a shower of popcorn flying toward him, followed by a tsunami of Pepsi.

"Loser!" says Peyton. "You blew it." She turns on her heel and walks away, fighting back the tears she'd never want him to see. What a mistake it was to allow someone in. She should have known she'd only end up getting hurt.

She takes three laps around the green, trying to calm herself down. Finally, figuring that Nathan's long gone if he knows what's good for him, she gets some more popcorn and sodas and works her way back to Brooke and Rusty. The music's started, and she can't see why she should miss the show.

Brooke gives her a concerned look, but Rusty is monopolizing her attention so anything more will have to wait. That's fine with Peyton. She doesn't want to talk about it now, anyway. She sits back in her seat, legs outstretched and arms folded, glowering at the stage.

The first band is just okay. Nothing special — they do a cover of some old Aerosmith tune. Next is an old guy who hobbles out with a cane, then sits down and plays some awesome ragtime piano. The crowd loves it and starts clapping along.

"Not bad for a crip" is Rusty's comment. Brooke elbows him, giggling. He tickles her, and she giggles some more. She spiked her soda with a big slug from a flask Rusty handed her, and she's feeling happy.

The third act is a little girl who does gymnastics to "God Bless America." Rusty gives her a big hand, but he's still making comments under his breath. Brooke, getting happier by the minute as she gulps her soda, pretends to shush him.

Peyton isn't exactly concentrating on the show, but she can't help paying attention when the announcer says that the fourth act is going to sing from the wings because "it's the little lady's first time on stage and she's kinda shy." He introduces her as Ms. Anonymous.

When the singer starts, a cappella, everybody seems to sit up and quiet down. Her voice is sweet and true, and the words to the song are poignant.

"I'm seein' it all through a haze," she sings, "moonlit nights and morning rays. But I'm too beat, too long on my feet, workin' my way through the dog days of summer. . . ."

After one verse, the crowd is with her. They're

listening — some are even clapping along. Peyton thinks there's something familiar about the voice, but she can't place it.

Then Rusty starts in. "What, she can't afford a guitar?" he says, loudly enough so that a few people nearby turn to glare at him. "What?" he mouths to Brooke. He grins. "She's probably ugly as hell, that's why she doesn't want to show herself. A total mongrel."

This time, Brooke shushes him for real. "I want to hear this," she says. "She's good!"

Rusty sits back and looks at her in disbelief. "Did you just shush me?" he asks.

Brooke nods and holds a finger up to her lips. "C'mon, Rusty," she whispers. "The song's almost over."

"I can't believe you're shushing me," Rusty says, still staring at her like she just grew an extra head.

"And I can't believe what a jerk you're being," Brooke says, without stopping to think.

It all happens so fast after that.

Rusty brings up the back of his hand and

smacks her across the cheek. "Don't talk to me like that, bitch!" he says.

Brooke sits back in her seat, holding a hand to her reddening face, stunned.

The crowd around them gasps.

And Peyton launches herself at Rusty, screaming at the top of her lungs. She comes at him fingernails first, scratching at his face and eyes.

"Yo, yo, yo!" Rusty says, grabbing her wrists.

He's laughing.

Peyton bends her face down and bites his hand — hard.

"Yow!" he yells, jumping up. "Bitch!"

By then, nobody much is listening to the final chorus of the song. A crowd has gathered around Brooke. That guy Mouth from the basketball court is holding her, rocking her gently as he tells her in a soothing voice that she's gonna be okay.

Rusty still has Peyton by the wrists when Whitey Durham materializes out of nowhere. "I'd advise you to let go of that girl," he drawls quietly, his bulk lending weight to his words. "And after that, I'd advise you to get your raggedy ass out of this town and never show yourself here again."

Rusty's shoulders slump. "I was just —" he begins, but Whitey interrupts.

"Now!" he says. "Go."

Rusty slinks off, his exit accompanied by applause — both for Whitey's words and for the singer's song, which has just ended.

Labor Day

MONDAY:
WARM–UP: STRETCH HAMSTRINGS, CALVES, ACHILLES, QUADS, LOWER BACK
SLOW RUN: 4 MILES TO KWIK–STOP AND BACK
SPRINTS: 25 YDS X 10
STRENGTH TRAINING:
STRAIGHT LEG DEADLIFT, BACK EXTENSION, BENCH PRESS (UP TO 155!), INCLINE CHEST FLY, BICEPS CURLS, FRENCH PRESS, WRIST CURLS, SQUATS, LUNGES, ABDOMINALS
SHOOTING DRILLS: LAYUP, JUMP SHOT, THREES

entry, Nathan's training diary

Nathan grunts as he replaces the twenty-five-pound barbells on the weight rack. He wipes his face with the crusty towel he's been using all summer, which he keeps forgetting to wash.

There's a slight, chilly breeze wafting in through the open window. It reminds Nathan that preseason practices will begin soon. That's how Nathan sees the year: Instead of spring, summer, winter, fall, it's postseason, off-season, preseason, basketball season. For so long, his life has been defined by basketball, starting way back with junior league.

He thinks back to those days and remembers how all the other kids — except one — were dribbling the ball with both hands. Nathan was way beyond that: Dan had put a basketball in his crib when he was six months old and had taught him how to make a free throw by the time he was three.

The other kid who dribbled with one hand? Nathan strains a little, trying to remember his face. Then it comes to him: It was Lucas. So — once upon a time, he played ball with the guy. His brother.

Interesting.

"You look deep in thought," says Dan, coming into the weight room. He checks Nathan's training diary and nods in approval.

Nathan shrugs.

"Girl trouble?" Dan grabs a pair of dumbbells and lies down on the bench to do some flies.

"Not exactly," Nathan says, although he does have girl trouble. Peyton has barely spoken to him for over two weeks now, ever since she caught him flirting with that girl Darlene. Not that he was flirting. He wasn't! He was just talking — what's wrong with that? But Peyton has been acting like she caught him in bed with the chick.

"Forget her," Dan advises, sticking to the idea of girl trouble. "She's not worth it."

Nathan looks at his father. He feels like saying, "What do you know about it?" Or even, "Advice from an expert?" Between the pregnant girl he left behind and the wife who's never around, Dan's not exactly a role model for successful relationships.

But Nathan doesn't say anything. He just goes back to his lunges. *The fact is,* he thinks as he works his quads over and over, *Peyton is worth it.* He misses her like crazy, even if she does drive him crazy sometimes. And if he wants her back, he's going to have to prove how much he cares.

*   *   *

"Ugh! Don't remind me!" Brooke shields her eyes from the marquee sign outside the high school. WELCOME BACK, STUDENTS! it says.

She and Peyton are out in the Comet, taking their final cruise of the summer. They're slugging their 7-Eleven Slurpees and eating Gummi Worms as they do the Tour de Tree Hill, checking out all the hot spots. The mix Peyton burned for the occasion is turned up high, and the car is rocking as both girls sing along with the Stones.

"Let's spend the night together, now I need you more than ever!" they wail along with Mick.

Brooke is loving it. She knows Peyton made this mix with her in mind, so it's not too heavy on the punk stuff. She definitely appreciates not having to listen to that noise. "Wouldn't it be great if we could just take off, do a long road trip?" she asks, shouting over the music.

"I'm down with that," says Peyton. "Next stop, Santa Fe!" She pretends to jerk the wheel to the right, grinning maniacally.

"Whoo-hoo!" cries Brooke. "We can find us some

cowboys out there!" She bounces in her seat. "Forget about Nathan and Rusty, we'll be hangin' with the bronco busters and bull riders."

Peyton lets loose with a "Whoo-hoo" of her own, but it's a little lame.

Brooke notices. "You're not over him, are you?" she says, meaning Nathan. "Not ready for Cowboy Slim?"

Peyton shakes her head. "Guess not," she admits. "I don't know what it is about the boy, but I do miss him."

As if on cue, the Stones break into "Miss You."

"So what are you going to do about it?" Brooke asks, bopping to the beat.

Peyton shrugs. "Get over it?" she asks. "I mean, if he's not willing to talk about it, neither am I. One of us has to make the first move, and it's not going to be me." She's too proud to admit she might have overreacted. Anyway, it's not just that one incident with the redhead. It's also that she's tired of their bickering. And she's had it with their make-up and breakup pattern. How many times can they go through that?

"I just hope you guys are on speaking terms by the time hoops season starts," Brooke says. "It's not gonna be pretty if the cheerleader is ragging on the team captain instead of cheering for him."

"Ugh, cheerleading," Peyton says. Every year she goes through the same thing, questioning whether she really wants to be on the squad. There's a lot she loves about cheering: the excitement, the athleticism, the way the squad works together like a team. But there's a lot she hates about it, too. The whole image thing, for one. She knows how people view cheerleaders, and she resents it. She's no airhead/slut/Valley girl, and she doesn't like being pigeonholed. "When does practice start?"

"Next week," Brooke tells her. "Gonna be there?"

Peyton shrugs. "Probably," she admits.

"Better be," Brooke says. "You keep the whole thing interesting."

Peyton steers the Comet around the town green, one of their favorite cruising routes. Both girls are quiet. They're remembering what happened at that spot a couple of weeks ago.

"Did I ever thank you properly for attacking that scumball?" Brooke asks lightly.

"About a zillion times," Peyton answers.

"Really, thank you," Brooke says seriously. "He was bad news, and I knew it. I just couldn't bring myself to break up with him. I guess I was scared to."

"And our lesson here is . . . ?" Peyton asks, grinning.

Brooke puts a finger to the side of her cheek, pretending to think. "Don't go out with scumballs, no matter how cute they are?" she asks finally.

"Very good," Peyton says. "If the alarm bells are ringing, evacuate the building immediately."

"I swear," says Brooke, holding up a hand in solemn vow, "to use better judgment next time."

Yeah, right, thinks Peyton. But she just smiles at her friend. Then, from inside her jacket pocket, her phone rings. It's the "espionage" ring tone, the one she assigned to Nathan. She and Brooke look at each other.

"Gonna answer?" Brooke asks. She's heard that ring before.

Peyton shakes her head. Then she reaches for the phone. Then she stops herself. "Aaah!" she yells, banging on the steering wheel. This is driving her crazy. She honestly doesn't know what to do. There are definitely some alarm bells in her head when it comes to Nathan. Should she follow her own advice and stay away?

The phone stops ringing.

Peyton lets out a big breath.

Two beats later, the "message waiting" ringtone sounds.

Peyton grabs the phone, dials in, and listens. She raises her eyebrows, and a tiny smile hits the corner of her mouth.

"What'd he say?" Brooke asks impatiently after Peyton hangs up.

Peyton doesn't answer. She just peels out, and she and Brooke head for home.

Ten minutes later, Peyton pulls up at her house and checks the mailbox out front, as directed by Nathan's voicemail. Inside is a bright red envelope. Peyton pulls it out and slits it open with her fingernail.

"What is it?" Brooke asks, looking over her shoulder.

"A treasure map," says Peyton. Her heart is thudding in her chest. Maybe things aren't over between her and Nathan after all. "I gotta go," she tells Brooke. "Want me to drop you at home?"

Soon the Comet is rocketing east on Route 126, toward the shore. The soundtrack has changed: Peyton has stuck in a different mix featuring Huffamoose, Silkworm, and the Pixies. Brooke would hate it, but Peyton is singing aloud — shouting aloud, really — to "Here Comes Your Man." She's smiling, too, and holding her left arm out the window, riding the currents of the wind as she blasts down the road.

She knows exactly where she's going: to the Scotts' beach house. The place she thought she'd be spending all kinds of time this summer. They didn't get there once, between Nathan's workout schedule and their breakups. She's never seen the house, but she's imagined it. She figures it'll be a smaller, funkier version of the Scotts' tastefully decorated mansion in Tree Hill. More of a cottage, probably.

She follows the map, which features red arrows showing the way. A left turn off the main drag takes her onto a quiet avenue that heads straight for the ocean. A right turn takes her onto a beautiful road that hugs the shoreline, with the beach on one side and grand old shingled houses lined up along the other. Beach roses tumble over the fence on the shore side, their brilliant pink blooms reminding Peyton suddenly of a scarf her mother used to wear. Long ago, long before she died. She probably had that scarf when Peyton was only six or so. Sometimes, old images of her mom come to Peyton like that, out of the blue. Sometimes, they make her sad. This time she's in too good a mood to dwell on it. Instead, she just smiles and says softly, "Hey, Mom." It feels like a little visit.

Peyton drives on, following the map. The houses start to sit farther apart, each one bigger than the next, with a bigger yard and more ocean frontage. That's when Peyton starts to wonder if she was wrong about the cottage.

Then she pulls up in front of the address noted on the map.

She was majorly wrong.

This place is a palace! If anything, it's even bigger than the Scotts' Tree Hill house. For a second, Peyton stares up at it, feeling intimidated. Then she takes a deep breath and checks the directions on the map. "Enter by the front door," it says in red. "Follow the trail to find your treasure." The treasure is marked with a big red heart.

Peyton takes off her sunglasses and tosses them on the front seat. She climbs out of the Comet. She walks up onto the broad porch and stares at the massive front door. Then, without knocking, she pushes carefully on it. It swings silently open, revealing an echoing front hall with gleaming, polished wood floors and a sweeping staircase.

And right up the middle of the stairs is a trail of beach rose petals.

Peyton smiles.

And she starts to climb.

At the top of the stairs, the trail of flowers turns right. Peyton follows it. Now her heart is really thudding. She hears music. It's Maroon 5.

The trail leads to a closed door. Tentatively, Peyton pushes it open and the music swells.

The room is filled with the warm, flickering light of dozens of white candles in every shape and size, set all around a beautiful, antique four-poster bed. The bed is covered with a white bedspread, and in the middle of it is a message, written in rose petals.

I'M SORRY, it says. I LOVE YOU.

Lying nestled in a heart made of more rose petals is a necklace, an intricate silver chain with a pearl pendant.

It's the most romantic thing Peyton has ever heard of, much less seen. And it's all for her.

"Peyton?"

She turns to see Nathan coming into the room.

She walks toward him.

And she melts into his arms.

*   *   *

Up on the roof at Karen's Cafe, Haley and Lucas are holding each other, too. It's a very different kind of hug, though. A victory hug, congratulating each other for making it through the summer. And for creating the very first hole of their soon-to-be-world-famous minigolf course.

They stand back to admire it. A life-size cardboard cutout of Britney Spears stands guard over the cup, smiling foxily as if she's completely unaware of how totally dorky she looks in her Dog Kart apron and dachshund hat. To get the ball into the hole, you have to putt up a long ramp with two curves in it, then tap the ball right between Britney's platform-wearing feet.

"What do you think?" asks Haley. "Par four?"

"No way," answers Lucas. "We're going to keep this course challenging. Par two at the most." He picks up a putter and takes a few practice shots. "So, you seem to be having a good time waitressing at the cafe."

"It rocks," says Haley happily. "The food rocks, your mom rocks, the customers rock. I love it."

"Speaking of rocking . . ." Lucas says. He's about to mention something, just casually, about how the voice of Ms. Anonymous at the Tree Hill Is Terrific show sounded awfully familiar.

But Haley cuts him off. "How's Skills doing?" she asks.

Lucas grins. "Great," he says. "He found himself a little apartment that's exactly midpoint between school and the river court. What could be more perfect?"

"Speaking of school . . ." Haley says. She's about to ask Lucas, just casually, if he's thinking of going out for the basketball team this year.

"Oops," says Lucas, checking his watch. "Gotta run. There's a game on down at the court, and you know how Mouth gets when people are late."

He gives her a quick squeeze, then stands back, holding her by the shoulders. They look at each other, and everything they didn't say passes between them. They don't need to spell it out. Bottom line? They'll always be there for each other, no matter what.

PART II

Before . . . and After

October 15

"Most people live ninety percent in the past, seven percent in the present, and that only leaves three percent for the future."

John Steinbeck, *The Winter of Our Discontent*

Big game at school tonight — at least that's what I hear. I try to ignore all the hype, but it's hard not to feel the buzz. So — I'll just have to get my own buzz, down at the river court.

entry, Lucas's journal

Game night. And a frosty nip is not the only thing in the air. There's also that feeling of anticipation, that breathless sense of not knowing what might happen.

Buses pull up to the main doors of Tree Hill High, their idling engines creating clouds of steam. Crowds of chattering, excited fans spill out of the buses and into the school. There's no hesitation about entering enemy territory — after all, there's safety in numbers. The visiting fans will flow, as if it's the natural order of things, into the bleachers on the left side of the gym. The bleachers on the right side are already filling up with Tree Hill fans. Girlfriends, little brothers, eager parents who have their regular seats.

The gym is warm, the air moist. The sound of bouncing balls reverberates off the walls, coupled with occasional grunts or laughs as the Ravens and their opposition warm up on opposite ends of the court.

The cheerleaders are nowhere in sight, but their handiwork covers the walls. SCOTT RULES! shouts one poster in neon pink and purple. GO RUBEN! screams another. TAKE IT, TIM!

Outside, a lone figure in a hooded sweatshirt dribbles a worn basketball through the parking lot. But instead of coming up the stairs and into the school, the dribbler moves on, past the idling buses, past the far parking lot, on toward the river.

Inside, things are heating up.

"Hope you brought your game," Nathan mutters

to the visiting point guard as they swing past each other at midcourt.

"Brought it, got it, takin' your ass to town," replies the boy, without breaking stride.

Nathan snorts. "Yeah, right," he says, mostly to himself.

The gym is packed by now. Team intros and tip-off are only minutes away. Nathan turns toward the basket and nonchalantly tosses in a three-pointer from outside the paint.

The crowd goes wild.

The game hasn't even started yet, and the crowd is going wild.

Nathan pretends not to hear the whistles, stomps, and cheers. But he can't quite hide a tiny, satisfied smile.

"Nathan," calls a voice from the sidelines.

It's Dan. He's been there since the first moment of warm-ups, as always. Pacing the sidelines like a tiger in a cage. Noticing every move Nathan makes.

Nathan turns, faces his father. Raises an eyebrow as if to say, yes?

"Remember," Dan says. "Twenty shots. No less."

"I got it, Dad," says Nathan. How could he not? Dan has been drilling it into his head all week.

Dan looks as if he's about to say something else, but just then Whitey interrupts. He doesn't bother smiling at Dan, much less looking at him. If there's anyone in Tree Hill who's not afraid of Dan Scott, it's Whitey Durham. Actually, Whitey's probably not afraid of a single soul on this earth. Why would he be? What could hurt him? Whitey's like a rhino, all tough hide and plodding, patient strength.

"Quit yakking and warm up," Whitey orders. He moves on. Nathan shrugs at Dan and trots back onto the court to toss one more ball through the hoop.

Meanwhile, out at the river court, the figure in the hooded sweatshirt arrives at the courts. The guys are already tossing it around. Skills is taunting Ferguson, dribbling toward him and away, spinning, faking left, faking right.

"And here he is," Mouth says, from his perch next to Edwards on the picnic table. He's speaking into a mic attached to an old-style tape recorder. "Lucas Scott. Scott is 137 and 3 going into tonight's contest."

Lucas bumps fists with Mouth and Edwards, then shucks his sweatshirt and heads onto the court.

Junk turns up next, stopping to give Mouth an affectionate smack upside the head.

Mouth grins. "And, as a special bonus, we're joined in the booth by Junk Moretti," he says into his mic.

"You don't have a booth," Junk points out.

"Actually," Edwards says suddenly, after thinking it over, "Lucas is 138 and 3."

Junk sniffs. "Jeez, Edwards," he says. "You can remember that, but you can't remember to run a bar of soap under your pits?"

"What?" Edwards asks, lifting an arm to sniff himself.

"You smell bad, man," Junk tells him. "Ripe."

Edwards looks at Mouth.

Mouth shrugs. Then he lifts an arm to check his own scent.

*   *   *

Back at the Tree Hill High gym, the game is about to start. Both teams are in their locker rooms. The crowd is waiting. The gym is almost quiet. Then the Raven cheerleaders burst through their locker room door and gallop onto the floor, yelling and stomping. Brooke and Peyton come through last, carrying a huge hoop covered in paper painted with the Ravens' symbol. The cheerleaders line up near the players' door. By now, the home crowd is going bananas, stomping and whistling.

"Ladies and gentlemen," says Eddie Mills, the announcer. "The Ravens!"

Nathan bursts through the paper, running at full speed for the court. The rest of the team piles out after him, through the shredded hoop. The crowd explodes.

Peyton rolls her eyes. They do this routine at every single home game. It's so lame, but it never fails to please. Tree Hill fans are easy to rile up.

The teams are introduced.

The anthem is sung.

Nathan tips off the ball, and the game is under way.

The Ravens are ahead by two, by five, by seven. They aren't playing their prettiest, but it doesn't seem to matter. Nathan has six shots under his belt, and Dan is looking as pleased as he ever does at a game.

Jake bobbles a pass and Nathan scoops it inbounds, grabs it, and works his way under the basket for a layup.

Whitey calls a time-out.

He's not happy.

"What in hell's going on out there?" he glowers.

Nathan smirks. "Relax, Whitey. We're up by nine."

Whitey doesn't relax. He rubs his neck. Ponders. Then he turns to Tim.

"Tim," he says. "Go in for Nathan."

Nathan looks down and away. He glances at his father. Sure enough, that vein in Dan's temple is throbbing.

Nathan takes his time walking to the end of the

bench. He checks out Peyton, down by the baseline with the other cheerleaders. She shrugs and blows him a kiss.

Whitey walks over and starts talking. He keeps his back to Nathan the whole time. "What'd I tell you about this?" he asks. "I don't care if we're up by five or fifty. I'm still the coach. You understand? This is my team, not yours."

Nathan's still gazing at Peyton. He likes the way her cheerleading top hugs her chest. He wonders which bra she's wearing. The pink one? The lacy white one?

Whitey turns to glare at Nathan. Nathan meets his eyes. "Whatever you want to believe," he says.

Whitey starts to pace. Ten minutes on the clock later, the Ravens are going down, struggling against a full-court press. At midcourt, they turn the ball over. The visitors race past a sagging Whitey and a sagging scoreboard.

Whitey looks at the clock. He paces. He rolls up a program in his huge, leathery hands.

Another steal.

Another score for the visitors.

The Tree Hill fans are quiet now. The air in the gym feels close, oppressive, like summer air before a storm.

Whitey paces. Finally, he arrives at the end of the bench. He stands there for another twenty seconds on the clock, twisting the program as he watches the visitors rally.

Finally, his broad, impassive back still toward Nathan, he speaks. "Go on," he says, so quietly that only Nathan can hear him.

A slow smile spreads across Nathan's face. He takes his time tightening his laces, then he heads for the scorer's table and waits for the buzzer. He saunters onto the court, and the crowd almost seems to sigh with relief. When he accepts the ball from the ref and inbounds, the storm breaks and the heavy air lifts.

It's Nathan's team. Nathan knows it, the fans know it.

Whitey knows it.

*　　*　　*

Nathan's not the only Scott son on a roll. Down at the river court, Lucas waits for Ferguson to set a pick. Then, calmly, gracefully, he drains a three-pointer. Skills and Junk don't look happy.

"That makes it 14–13, game point for Team Scott," Mouth says into his mic. He speaks urgently, quietly, like a sportscaster at a golf tournament. "For those of you at home," he adds, "Lucas wears black shorts tonight with his traditional white high-tops."

Edwards, the color man for the night, chimes in. "He's currently playing without a show contract, Mouth."

On the court, Lucas checks the ball and slings it to Fergie. Then, effortlessly, he runs Junk into Skills, springing free twenty-five feet from the rim.

Mouth is loving the action. "Luke flashes through the paint," he narrates. "Fergie finds him out top —"

Lucas releases the shot, apparently unaware of the charging Skills and Junk.

"— Scott for the game!" Mouth crows.

High fives and hugs all around. Lucas slips on his sweatshirt and pulls up the hood.

"I had you tonight, Luke," Junk tells him.

"Junk," Skills says, overhearing. "He was killing you."

"So?" Junk asks.

Lucas just smiles. "You played well tonight, Junk," he says. "I had to work for it." He bumps fists with Junk. "You, too, Fergie," Lucas says with a nod at his teammate. Then he turns to Skills. "Skills, you were horrible."

Everybody cracks up.

"All right," Lucas says, grinning at Skills to show he was only ragging on him. "See you in the morning!" He sticks in his earpods, fires up his MP3, pulls up his hood, and starts off at a slow jog, dribbling his ancient ball.

The guys watch him go.

Skills rolls his eyes at Junk. "You had him," he says.

The Tree Hill High gym is empty now, silent. Game over. The Ravens fans flood out of the place, high on victory. The visitors, who at halftime could almost taste a win, trickle out quietly to board their buses.

One of which is missing.

Two miles away, a wildly grinning Nathan pilots the bus along a country road. Outside the bus, all is quiet and peaceful. Inside, it's a different world. A party. There's a keg in back, and Jake is pouring for all comers. Beer sloshes in plastic cups as Nathan careens around a corner. Ruben and his girlfriend are all over each other in one seat, and another couple in back of them are nearly naked, the girl's bra hanging over the seat.

Tim, riding shotgun, crows into Nathan's ear. "Tell me we didn't just steal a school bus! 'Cause this feels like we just stole a school bus."

"C'mon, man," Nathan says. "We just borrowed it."

Melody, a pretty, slightly drunk girl, pops up behind the driver's seat. "So, Nathan," she says, "where's Peyton?"

Nathan eyes Melody in the rearview. "Who knows?" he asks. "Why?"

The bus is hurtling toward a railroad crossing, but Nathan doesn't notice. All he notices right now is Melody's intense, dark gaze.

Melody leans in and plants a long, sloppy kiss on Nathan's lips.

Tim sees the freight train screaming toward the crossing. "Look out!" he shouts, grabbing the wheel.

Nathan detaches himself from Melody, swivels back to face front, and stands on the brakes. The bus shudders to a stop.

Across town, Peyton is bombing along in the Comet. She wanted nothing to do with the bus-jacking, nothing to do with the whole idiotic Ravens scene. The guys are nearly intolerable after they win a game like that. Like little boys, so pleased with themselves. And the other cheerleaders just encourage it.

Not Peyton. She'd rather celebrate by herself — or rather, with the Foo Fighters. It's a mix she made herself. All the best, most head-banging tunes. Where is that CD? Without letting up on the gas, Peyton turns to rummage in the backseat. Aha! There it is, underneath her sketchpad. Peyton grabs it, shoves it into her stereo, cranks the volume, and looks back at the road — just in time to see a hooded figure about to cross in front of her speeding car. She slams on the brakes.

The Comet slides, fishtails, and comes to a stop.

Lucas tosses back his hood and glares at Peyton. Freakin' Hill girls think they own the world.

Peyton glares back at Lucas. Spacey idiot almost got himself killed.

Lucas pulls out his earpods.

Peyton rolls down her windows.

Same song.

Same verse.

Perfectly synchronized.

Too weird.

Peyton blinks. Then she holds up her hand. Extends her middle finger.

Lucas recoils. Pulls up his hood. And moves off into the darkness, dribbling his ball.

Back at the tracks, Nathan is shaking his head as he watches the train scream by. He can't help smiling. As usual, his luck trumps all. Nathan Scott is not destined to end his life in some stupid, gory crash on the railroad tracks.

The caboose rumbles past. And the grin drains from Nathan's face as he looks across the tracks to the squad car sitting on the other side. An officer, arms folded across his chest, is standing outside the vehicle.

Oops.

Nathan knows he's blown it. At the very least, he'll be suspended from the team. Nathan immediately thinks of his dad. How will Dan react? He'll be more upset about the lost opportunities for Nathan's career point total than about the fact that Nathan nearly got creamed by a train.

The officer gestures for everyone to get off the bus. The team piles off, quiet now, chastened. One guy belches, but nobody laughs.

They line up, eyes on the ground. The cop shines his spotlight on each of them in turn, looking them over. He shakes his head, disgusted, as he moves down the line.

Nathan's brain is in overdrive. Should he try to run? Give a fake name? Right. Like there's one single resident of Tree Hill who doesn't know who he is.

But, as it turns out, none of that is necessary.

When the cop's light hits Nathan, and Tim standing next to him, it lingers only momentarily. Nathan is blinded for a moment. Then the light swings away and he can see the cop again. The cop is waving a hand at him. It's the universal sign for "get outta here."

Nathan doesn't need to be told twice. Smirking, he grabs Tim and takes off.

October 16

TUESDAY:
WARM—UP: WHO NEEDS IT?
SLOW RUN: YEAH, RIGHT.
SPRINTS: WHY BOTHER?
STRENGTH TRAINING: WHATEVER.
THE HELL WITH IT. OUR SEASON'S DOG MEAT, ANYWAY. I DON'T
KNOW WHAT THE BIG DEAL IS — SO WE STOLE A BUS! IT'S NOT LIKE
WE KILLED SOMEBODY. BUT YOU JUST KNOW THEY'RE GOING TO
MAKE A HUGE CASE OUT OF IT. THE GUYS ARE WAY BUMMED. I GUESS
I AM, TOO. BUT MAYBE . . . NOT TOTALLY?

entry, Nathan's training diary

The next day they make a big production out of
the whole thing, at the school library. The place is
packed with all the varsity players, all their parents,
the principal, and a handful of cops — including
Chief Wayman, and the one who waved Nathan
away. Whitey's there, too — over by the door, as if he
wants nothing to do with the scene.

Principal Turner is talking. *Blah, blah, blah* is all Nathan hears. Then he sees Dan glaring at him, and he pretends to listen.

"Some of you parents," says Turner, "see this latest incident as tomfoolery. A little prank. Personally, I see a little breaking and entering." He turns to look at Chief Wayman. "Chief Wayman sees possession and consumption by minors — and a smidgen of grand theft auto."

Nathan can see that vein throbbing in Dan's temple. Not a good sign.

"That said," continues Turner, "I think it's time we send a message. Call it long overdue." He looks down at the list in his hand, then around at the crowd. "The following players were not involved and will not be reprimanded," he says, a little more loudly than necessary. "Jake Jagielski, Ruben Gutierrez, Tim Smith . . ."

Nathan holds his breath.

". . . and Nathan Scott."

Nathan sighs with relief. But the vein in Dan's temple doesn't disappear.

"As for the rest of you," Turner goes on sternly, "all players involved are suspended from extracurricular activities, specifically basketball, for the rest of the season."

Nathan follows Dan's glance and watches as Whitey, who is wearing a strange, small smile, disappears through the door.

Whitey makes it almost all the way back to his office in the gym before Dan catches up to him.

"You just walk away," Dan says, tight-lipped.

Whitey turns calmly. "Dan Scott," he says.

Dan is furious. "Half the team is suspended, Nathan'll get triple-teamed the rest of the year, and you say nothing."

Whitey shrugs. "Nobody asked me," he answers.

"Well," says Dan, barely controlling an urge to reach out and choke the complacent coach. "I'm asking you now."

Whitey meets Dan's eyes. That small smile reappears. "The inmates will not run the asylum," he says.

That nearly sends Dan around the bend. He

narrows his eyes, takes a threatening step forward. "What's this really about, huh?" he asks. "It's not about beer or buses or any of that nonsense. It's about you, me, and Nathan."

Whitey doesn't flinch. "C'mon now, Danny," he says. "It hasn't been about you since the buzzer sounded on your senior season. How 'bout you let it go and leave the game to Nathan?" He pretends not to notice the way Dan's face goes white with fury. In fact, he turns and starts to walk away.

"You're despicable," Dan says to Whitey's back. "You know that? Letting the dreams of good kids just vanish. You're so full of crap."

Whitey doesn't turn around. "Comes with old age, Danny," he says lightly as he pads off down the hall. "Constipation."

That night, Lucas meets the guys at the river court. Mouth and Edwards perch on the picnic table, yakking with Fergie and Skills. Lucas takes shot after shot, with Junk retrieving and lobbing the ball back to him. Junk is dishing about the bus incident, old classmates, girls he's "heard things" about. Lucas keeps shooting, trying to ignore the chatter.

Skills changes the subject. "So, Luke, whatcha reading these days?"

Lucas takes the question straight, even if Skills didn't mean it that way. "Steinbeck," he answers, sinking the seventh three-pointer in a row, "*The Winter of Our Discontent.*"

"Let's hear a little," says Skills.

Lucas looks at him. "Nah," he says.

"C'mon, man," Skills says, serious now. "You know I read vicariously through you."

Lucas sinks another shot. Nothing but net. Junk returns the ball. Then, holding the ball, Lucas turns to Skills. "'What a frightening thing is the human,'" he quotes, "'a mass of gauges and dials and registers, and we can read only a few, and those perhaps not accurately . . .'" He turns, sets up to shoot again as he continues the quote.

He's interrupted by the sound of screeching tires. He glances toward the road and sees that car. The Comet. Peyton's ride, blasting past. He lets go of the ball. It sails toward the net, just like all the others. But then it seems to take a sudden dive. It bangs hard off the rim. First miss of the night.

"Peyton Sawyer," Edwards says thoughtfully.

Junk grins. "You guys see her webcam?" He doesn't wait for an answer. "It's in her bedroom. I heard she's naked on it, like, all the time."

Head-shakes all around.

"What?" Junk says. "I hear things."

Lucas steps to the line again, ready to shoot. "I saw her the other night," he says casually. "She almost ran me over."

"She's pretty fine, huh, Luke?" Skills asks.

"She's all right," says Lucas. He ignores the snickers. "C'mon," he says. "Let's shoot for teams."

At that very moment, Keith Scott is knocking softly on the door of Whitey's gym office.

Whitey doesn't hear the first knock. He's lost in thought, listening to an old, familiar song playing on his radio and stroking a big old tabby cat that's camped out on his lap. Whitey is gazing at a picture of Camilla. His face is a map of loneliness.

Keith knocks again and pokes his head into the office. Whitey suddenly looks a lot happier. "Keith Scott," he says. "Whaddaya know?"

"Hey, Coach," Keith says, pushing the door all the way open and walking in. "Got a second?"

"Got a lot of seconds," Whitey says wryly. "Haven't you heard?"

"Yeah, I heard." Keith pulls a flask of whiskey out of his jacket pocket and raises an eyebrow.

Whitey pushes his coffee mug toward Keith. "Just a little," he says.

Keith pours a slug.

"A little more," Whitey says. He doesn't pick up the mug until Keith has topped it off. Then he takes a long sip. His eyes go wet. "Saw your little brother today," he tells Keith. "Danny. Called me despicable. Said I crush the dreams of young men."

Keith snorts. "And was he talking about Nathan or himself, do you figure?"

"Oh, both, I suppose," says Whitey. He takes another gulp from his mug. He watches as Keith looks up at an old team photo on the wall. Both Scott brothers are in it: Nathan front and center and Keith hovering around in the background.

"What'd you average for me that season?" asks Whitey, nodding toward the photo.

Keith grins. "'Bout five fouls and six beers a night." It never really bothered him that he couldn't play ball the way Dan could.

"Well, at least you were consistent," Whitey says, grinning back.

There's a brief silence. Then Keith gets to the point of his visit. "You know Lucas plays," he says.

"Dan's other son," Whitey acknowledges. He and Keith have never really talked about it.

"Karen's son," Keith corrects the coach. "Dan's on the birth certificate, but that's about it."

He's not telling Whitey anything Whitey — and everybody else in Tree Hill — doesn't know. "Plays where?" Whitey says, getting back to the point.

"Park near the river," says Keith.

Whitey grimaces. "C'mon now, Keith," he says. "You're not drinking with a street-ball fan, and you know it. These kids had any love for the game they'd be in the gym with the real players."

Keith tightens his lips. "You mean like Nathan?" He puts down his glass. "Take a drive with me, Coach."

Ten minutes later, they're sitting in the dark car watching Lucas play. He's flowing up and down the court, making it look easy. Junk can't get a hand on the ball as Lucas drains jumper after jumper.

Whitey doesn't say much for a few minutes. Finally, he speaks up. "What's his head like?" he asks.

"He's smart as hell out there," Keith responds immediately.

"How 'bout when he's not out there?" Whitey asks.

Keith has an answer for that, too. "He's always out there. Wrestling with a past he had nothing to do with."

On the court, Lucas draws a double team and finds Fergie for an easy layup. Whitey watches, rubbing his neck.

"Let's say I'm interested," the old coach says. "And I'm not saying I am. Why put him through it?"

Keith thinks for a second. "He should know he's good," he says. "Not playground good, but good period. He could use that in his life."

"We all could use that in life," Whitey tells him.

"Yeah," Keith agrees. "But we had our shot."

Whitey looks at Keith. His curiosity gets the better of him. "So, you and Karen . . ."

"Friends," Keith says quickly. "I'm the kid's uncle. I'm in their lives." He looks out the window, looks back. "It is what it is." He pulls out his flask.

"You should go easy on the sauce," Whitey advises.

Keith starts to put the flask away.

Whitey grabs it. "I said *you* should." He takes a swig. "I remember when Danny came to me and told me Karen was pregnant," he says quietly. "Summer after their senior year." He slumps back in his seat. "I told him to honor his scholarship and go to college . . . but I knew Karen was pregnant. And I liked her. Maybe I was being too much coach and not enough human being."

Keith shakes his head. "Well, Dan's version of the

story is that he felt trapped by Karen. That falling in love with Deb that first semester in college changed everything." He looks out at Lucas again, shrugs. "This much I do know," he finishes. "You did Karen a favor. And Lucas, too. Now you can do me one."

If Lucas noticed Keith at the park, he doesn't mention it to Karen when he heads home that night. He finds his mom in the cafe, wiping down the counter. Lucas flips the sign to CLOSED as he walks in the door. "Hey, Mom," he says, stepping behind the counter to give her a kiss.

"Hey, honey." Karen looks tired. She always does by ten.

"You change your hair?" Lucas asks, studying her.

"If by 'change' you mean dragging a brush through it, then sure."

"Well, it looks nice," Lucas tells her.

Just then there's a squeal from over by the tables. "Ew!" It's Haley, cleaning up for the night. She comes over to Lucas, holding out a magazine. "It's all sticky. Were you reading this?"

Lucas smiles down at her. "I don't know, Haley. Is that the 'Why Do I Hang Out with These People?' issue? 'Cause you're on the cover of that, right?"

"Actually," Haley comes right back at him, "it's the 'My Best Friend Is an Idiot' issue, and — " She flips open the mag and pretends to spot a picture. "Oh, there you are!"

Karen, meanwhile, has brought a couple of bowls of chili over to a table near the window. "Haley, you want to join us?" she asks, not quite meaning it. She wants to sit with her son, hear about his day.

But Haley jumps at the invitation. "Hell, yes," she says. "You know my mom can't cook." She goes over to the chili pot and ladles herself a bowl.

"So, honey," Karen says to Lucas. "How was your day?"

Just then, Haley plops down at the table. "Good!" she answers, oblivious to the looks Lucas and Karen exchange. "I mean, good is relative, right? I mean, considering a third of the world is starving, which still doesn't change the fact that I'm clumsy as hell." She rattles on without stopping for breath. "Did I tell you I fell down today? Yeah. Slipped off the curb and completely bit it. Facedown, ass in the air . . ."

"Haley," Karen interrupts.

"Oops," says Haley. "Too graphic? Too graphic. I'll be quiet."

"So, Luke," Karen says, moving on. "I got you something."

"Actually," Haley jumps in again, "I found it. I mean, sort of. I mean, not that I was looking specifically for you, which would imply some hideous Joey loves Dawson scenario and completely creep me out. It's just that we saw it and — oh, just give him the book."

Karen slides a book over the table to Lucas. He checks out the cover. "*Julius Caesar*," he says. "Shakespeare."

Karen nods and tries to quote. "'There's a tide in the affairs of men . . .' something like that."

"Nice," says Haley. She holds out a fist. Karen bumps it.

Lucas is still looking at the book. "Wow. Thanks, guys," he says. He means it.

Haley breaks the moment. "Whatever," she says. "If that's what you're into."

The mood's a little different over at Peyton's. She's huddled in her closet/studio, her expression as black as its walls. The soundtrack? "Your Boyfriend Sucks," by the Ataris, at top, bone-rattling volume. Peyton is PhotoShopping an image of a smiling guy with a snow shovel, pasting it onto another image of a tomb full of skulls. He's just another happy skull shoveler. Peyton's webcam captures the action, or lack thereof, for anyone who might be cruising her site.

"What are you wasting your time at now?" It's Nathan.

Anybody watching would see a tight smile cross Peyton's face. "I didn't hear you come in," she says.

Nathan rolls his eyes. "Imagine that," he says, reaching over to pull the needle off the record. "Ya know, nobody listens to this crap," he adds.

Peyton leaves her skull-man behind and exits the closet, leaning in the doorway to look at Nathan.

"So I waited for you tonight," she feels compelled to say.

Nathan shrugs. "The guys wanted to tip a few," he says, like that's an answer.

"Did you even think to let me know?" Peyton hates the way she sounds. She hates this whole conversation. But somehow she can't stop herself.

"That's why I came by," Nathan covers smoothly. "You wanna come?"

"With the guys." Peyton's voice is flat.

"And me," Nathan reminds her.

"And the guys." Peyton isn't letting up.

Nathan sends a breath upwards. "Ya know, Peyton, I'm getting real tired of this. I came by to spend time with you."

"Yeah," says Peyton. She's tired of it, too. "Me and half the team."

"Whatever," Nathan says. Now he's pissed. "You wanna be a bitch? Fine. Just sit in your closet and listen to your loser rock. I'll see you tomorrow."

Peyton's not about to let him have the last word. "How about don't see me tomorrow?" she spits out.

"Fine by me," Nathan says. "Like I don't have options."

He knows that's a stupid thing to say. Of course he has options. So does Peyton. Either of them could have anyone they chose. But they've chosen each other.

He glares at her for one more beat. Then he hangs his head. "I'm sorry. Most of the guys are suspended so it's, like, this stupid bonding thing." He looks at her out of the corner of his eyes, puts on his pleading, puppy-dog face. "I wish it was just you and me, but I wanted you to come anyway to make it more bearable. Okay?"

Peyton's face doesn't change.

Nathan ratchets up the puppy-face.

She steps into his arms.

The puppy grins and holds her tight.

October 17

"We are not permitted to choose the frame of our destiny. But what we put into it is ours."

— Dag Hammerskold (1905–1961), Swedish statesman, Secretary-General of the United Nations

Why do things always have to change? I was happy before – or at least content. Now? Everything's different. How do I sort it all out: people's expectations, Mom's feelings, the chance to find out how good I really am, how good I could be. To discover my destiny.

entry, Lucas's journal

It's a glorious day. The library windows, cracked open to let in the fresh, crisp air, face out on the Tree Hill High School quad, where three venerable sycamores stretch bare limbs to a clear, blue December sky. It's the kind of day that makes you want to take off, hike the nearest mountain, fling open your arms to the world. Or something.

Where do you not want to be? Study hall. Until exactly eleven minutes after one, that is. A moment nobody who's in that room will ever forget. A moment that separates "before" from "after."

Just as the minute hand clicks past the two on the big clock over the door, Coach Durham — known as Whitey to every mother's son in Tree Hill, North Carolina — strides into the room.

"Scott!" he shouts.

Two heads turn in his direction.

One, darkly handsome and held high with a self-confidence bordering on arrogance.

The other, with golden waves framing a sensitive face and eyes that might have belonged to a fox struggling to escape from a trap.

"'Sup, Coach?" asks Nathan. He begins to pile his books together, getting ready to head to the gym. No doubt Whitey wants to talk to him about how the Ravens will handle defense in Friday's game.

"Not you," Whitey answers brusquely. He nods to the other boy, the blond. "You."

By now, everyone in the room is staring. At Whitey. At Nathan.

At Lucas.

Nathan is still looking at Whitey. His mouth hangs open. Whitey's eyes meet Nathan's with an even gaze. "You read a book or something," Whitey tells Nathan. Then he turns on his heel and leaves the room, not even checking to see if Lucas is following.

Slowly, Lucas gathers his things. Stands up. Darts a look at Nathan. And follows Whitey out of the room.

It's a little overwhelming, being in the gym. Lucas has worked hard to avoid the place. He may be the only guy in school who has never attended a Ravens game. The wood floor is polished and shining. The nets on the hoops look fresh and new, unlike the chain "nets" at the river court. The bleachers stand empty, awaiting the eager crowds. There's one folded white towel sitting on the home bench — a leftover from the last game? And there on the wall, up near the announcer's booth, is the big sign: WHITEY DURHAM FIELD HOUSE — HOME OF THE TREE HILL RAVENS.

As if there'd been any question about it.

This is Whitey's place.

And Lucas has been invited in.

His eyes continue to flick around the walls until he comes to the banner emblazoned with Dan Scott's ALL-TIME HIGH SCORING statistics. He flinches a little when he sees that.

Whitey is silent, gazing around as if seeing the place through Lucas's eyes. Finally, he speaks. "Nice, isn't it?" he asks. "Most people like their gyms loud, but I like it this way. Quiet. Clean. Like a church." He smiles. "Lotta praying done in here, anyway."

Lucas is still looking around. He hears Whitey, but he doesn't respond. Doesn't see the need to. Not yet.

Whitey likes the way the kid contains himself.

But it's time to get him talking. "You played in grade school," he says. "Why'd you quit?"

"I didn't." Lucas states the obvious.

Whitey isn't buying. "Well . . . four kids in the park isn't exactly basketball."

Lucas brings up his head, meets Whitey's eyes. "Then what do you think we're doing out there?"

Whitey shrugs, pretends to joke. "Maybe . . . planning a bank job?"

Lucas honors the joke with a half-smile.

Whitey sees that it's time to get to the point. "I got an opening in my lineup. Varsity. Chance of a life-time." He grabs a ball off the rack and tosses it to Lucas. "Whattaya say?"

Lucas looks down at the ball. It seems brand-new, at least compared to his. He rotates it in his hands. Then he takes another glance around the gym. "I say, those people who pray here? They're wasting their time." He looks up at the basket, and for a second he's almost tempted to shoot. But he doesn't. He looks back at Whitey. "God doesn't watch sports," he says. Then he drops the ball and heads toward the door. The echo of its bouncing follows him long after he leaves the gym.

In fact, it follows him all the way down to the river court that night. He's shooting free throws, trying to concentrate, while the other guys are doing their best imitation of the Spanish Inquisition. Word has traveled fast, and there's no way he can hide what happened.

"So, were you gonna tell us?" asks Skills.

"It's nothing," says Lucas.

Skills stares at him in disbelief. "Whitey asks you to play on the team and it's . . . nothing?"

"It's nothing because I'm not playing. Not with those guys." Lucas can't believe they don't get it.

"Luke," says Skills, "I've been guarding you almost every night since we were what, twelve? And I've won how many games?"

It's a rhetorical question, but Edwards can't help answering. "Seven," he says solemnly. "I mean, since I've been keeping stats."

Junk gives Edwards a look.

But Skills just shakes his head. "Seven," he says. "Seems like a waste to me."

Lucas bristles. "Well, it doesn't to me, okay? You guys ever think that maybe this is where we belong?"

Now it's Skills's turn to get mad. "No," he says. "This is where *we* belong. *You* never belonged here."

Lucas doesn't know quite how to take that. "Thanks a lot, Skills," he says finally. "Let's shoot for teams." He tosses the ball to his friend.

Skills tucks the ball under his arm. "You know, Luke," he says thoughtfully, "you're one of my best friends, and nothing's going to change that. But let's face it. We're not shooting for teams. We're shooting to be your excuse. And I don't want to be a part of that."

He stands there, looking at Lucas.

Behind him, the others stand in silent agreement.

Before. And after. Everything's already changed.

Over at the Scott palace, Nathan is working out. The Scott weight room is better outfitted than the school gym's. In a way, Nathan still likes the school weight room better. It has this funky feel, and there are other guys working out. Plus, there's no trophy case full of dozens of Dan's gleaming prizes. But if Dan doesn't see him doing his circuits, Dan doesn't believe they're getting done. So Nathan grunts it out alone at home, cranking the hip-hop until it drowns out everything else.

He's on the bench press when Dan walks in, looking agitated. The first thing he does is snap off the music. "Your mother phoned," he tells Nathan. "She'll be home next week. I didn't want to interrupt your workout." He checks the weights on the bar. "What're you slingin'?"

"'Bout one-sixty," Nathan says.

Dan nods. He reaches down, picks up two ten-pound weights, and slides them onto the bar. "So," he asks, his jaw tightening, "what do you know about Whitey inviting —"

"— your son to play?" Nathan finishes for him. Dan's eyes flash a warning. "Don't call him that."

"He has our last name, Dad," Nathan says. He huffs as he raps out a rep.

Dan tries another tack. "Nathan," he says, in his most I'm-trying-to-be-reasonable voice, "I know I haven't spoken much about this kid in the past, but the fact that he shares our last name was wishful thinking on his mother's part. We were young. Summer after high school. We made a mistake."

Nathan lets the bar back down on the supports. "You made a mistake, all right," he says. "The guy's a zombie."

Dan nods. "Okay," he says, as he adds a twenty-pound weight to each end of the bar.

Is that all he's going to say? Nathan can't believe it. "Well, it's kinda screwed up, Dad," he says. "People talk about it." He takes the bar off the supports, brings it down, and tries to push out a rep. It's not happening. Dan's loaded it up too much. Nathan tries again. No way.

Finally, Dan pulls the bar off his son's chest. "All right, get out of there," he says. Nathan gets up and

Dan takes his place. He pumps a couple reps, clearly making some kind of point. Then he sits up and wipes his face with a towel. "I want you to talk to this kid," he says. "Encourage him not to play."

Nathan stares at his father. What's the problem? Does Dan think this Lucas kid is a threat? "I'm not afraid of him," he says.

"Well, you should be," Dan says curtly. "We've worked too hard to have anyone coming in now. Disrupting the offense. Taking away shots." He wipes his face again, avoiding Nathan's eyes. "And anyway," he goes on, "this has more to do with Whitey and me than you."

He lies back on the bench and pumps out a few more reps. Sits up again. "I'll tell you all about it someday. For now, you go to this kid and you talk to him. And trust me when I tell you there's a bigger picture here, Nathan." Dan looks straight into Nathan's eyes. "Your picture." He wipes his face and tosses the towel to Nathan. "And this kid's not in it."

*   *   *

"This kid" is at home, trying on the Ravens jersey that he found in a big padded envelope propped against the front door. He didn't mean to put it on, but somehow Lucas couldn't help himself. He's checking out his reflection in the mirror when Karen passes his open bedroom door.

She takes him in. The familiar black-and-white jersey looks . . . right on him. She hates that. And she especially hates the way the name Scott is branded on it, in bold black letters across the back. She knows she shouldn't react. Lucas needs to do what he needs to do. But the sight of that jersey brings everything flooding back.

"Somebody left it at my door," Lucas tells her helplessly. He sees how it is for her. She looks as if someone punched her in the stomach.

Karen can't help herself. "Take it off," she says. She turns and goes downstairs.

A couple hours later, Lucas finds her on the porch, watching the setting sun turn the sky to liquid gold. "Mom," he says, sitting down next to her. "You okay?"

"Yeah," she says, even though she's not. "Do you know who left it?"

"Coach Durham," Lucas says. He looks down at his hands. "He asked me to play."

There's a silence. Karen takes a breath. "Maybe you should," she says, so quietly that it's like rain running down a window.

"Now you sound like Skills," Lucas says. "You know, those guys refused to play with me today. They said they didn't want to be my excuse."

Karen nods. "And how'd you feel about that?"

"Honestly?" Lucas asks. It's so great to talk to her. She — listens. "I was pissed. Those guys are supposed to be my friends."

"They are your friends," Karen says simply. She picks something up from the table next to her, slides it over to Lucas. It's a picture. "Remember this?"

Lucas grins in spite of himself. "My first leather basketball," he says. "That was the year Skills's father told us there was no Santa Claus."

Karen laughs. "Yep. I tried to talk you out of it. But then you said something I'll never forget. You said you felt bad for the kids who never figured it out, because when they grew up and had kids of their own, there wouldn't be gifts on Christmas morning."

Karen likes that memory. She slides an arm around Lucas's shoulders. "You're a good kid, Luke," she says softly. "But sometimes I feel like you're sitting out your life on account of me, and I don't want that for you." She looks into his eyes. "My past isn't your future. Okay?"

After a moment, Lucas nods. He sits with her for a while longer, just watching the sunset together without talking. Then he grabs his ball and heads for the river court. If the guys won't play, he'll shoot alone. He needs it.

It's dark now. Nathan and Tim drive through town. "So," says Tim, who's wondering why Nathan picked him up, "your pops finally mentioned the bastard spawn. They say he's got game. Maybe we could use him."

Nathan swivels to look at Tim. This guy is supposed to be his friend? "Please," he says. "I can get us to State with three blind guys and a cripple. Practically what I got now with you and what's left."

"Nice," says Tim. "So what are you gonna do?"

Nathan hauls the steering wheel hard to the right. "Let's go to the park," he says, as if he's just decided.

A few minutes later, Nathan pulls up next to the river court. The other Scott in town is out on the court, sinking shot after shot. Lucas is either so focused on his shooting that he doesn't notice Nathan's arrival . . . or maybe he's so focused on pretending not to notice that he succeeds. Either way, he doesn't quit shooting until Nathan stalks out onto the court and retrieves his most recent swish.

"Nice shot," says Nathan. "Think you can hit it against a double team, down by two, a packed house telling you ya suck?"

Lucas doesn't answer. Why bother? He just stands, waiting for the ball.

Nathan looks over at Tim. "How about with just two people telling you ya suck?" There's something a little dangerous in his voice. He's a little close to the edge. Nathan plays well on the edge.

"What do you want?" Lucas asks. The question is sincere.

"What do *I* want?" Nathan repeats. "What do *you* want?" He starts dribbling the ball, moving in a slow circle around Lucas. "I mean, other than my girlfriend and my spot in the lineup?"

You can practically hear Tim suck in a breath. Nathan's eyes flick over to Tim and back to Lucas. He's enjoying this, and it's even a little better with an audience.

"Look," Nathan says, "none of us wants you on the team. I don't want you, the guys don't want you, and my girlfriend sure as hell doesn't want you."

Lucas still isn't speaking.

Nathan crosses over his dribble once, then again, then fakes a chest pass at Lucas.

Lucas doesn't flinch.

"But here's the deal." Nathan is getting ready to deliver his exit line. "You and me. One-on-one. You name the time and place." He dribbles one more time. "If you win," he finishes, "I'll quit the team. But if I win — you crawl back into your hole and remember your place in all this."

Palming the ball, Nathan extends it toward Lucas. "Time and place, baby. Time and place." Then he swings around and chucks the ball deep into the darkness beyond the court. Without another word, he turns and swaggers off toward his car.

October 18

What I'm listening to today: "Chrome" by
Matthew Ryan
     Things can be broken and they
can be beautiful. Metal, cold, twisted.
Shiny, strong, silver. Hearts, minds,
people ... what do you do with a heart
made of chrome?

    entry, Peyton's blog

    Peyton is blasting down River Road in the Comet,
wondering if it's possible to drive fast enough to out-
run all your worries, your doubts, your fears.

    She feels like something big is about to
happen — but she's not sure exactly what it is.
Things are changing, there's no doubt about it. Do
those "things" include her feelings for Nathan? Her
feelings for — Lucas?

    Peyton shakes her head, as she often does when

the thought — or the image — of Lucas enters her mind.

She just wishes everything would stop, freeze, just as it is.

At just that moment, when she's wishing, the Comet sputters, coughs, and backfires. Then, the engine no longer humming, it rolls to a stop.

"Damn!" Peyton tries the ignition.

Nothing.

Be careful of what you wish for. . . .

Lucas knows he's going to have to tell Haley. He tells her everything. And, frankly, he values her opinion. "Walk me to the body shop?" he asks after school the next day. He's already a little late for work, but Keith never gives him a hard time.

They take one of their favorite shortcuts through a quiet, grassy little alley. Lucas tells her about the gauntlet Nathan has thrown down.

"So, Nathan challenged you. You gonna play him?" she asks.

Lucas shrugs. "I don't know. It's not like I have anything to prove."

Haley bites her lip. "Yeah, I guess." But then a spark comes into her eye. "But don't you just want to show 'em sometimes? You know, just — whoa!" Suddenly they've come upon a huge flock of pigeons. The cooing birds swirl up into flight, swooping all around Haley and Lucas.

"Damn, what is this?" Haley yells, batting them away. "Last week I got attacked by a flock of crows."

Lucas can't help grinning as he watches Haley defend herself from the birds.

"I'm serious!" she says.

Finally, the birds settle back down. They were never all that interested in assaulting Haley, anyway.

"By the way," Lucas says, as they continue their walk. "It's a murder."

"Huh?" Haley looks at him, confused.

"More than one crow is a murder," Lucas explains.

Like that clears it up. "I don't know what the hell you're talking about," Haley says.

Lucas looks up, as if trying to remember. "A parliament of owls. An exultation of larks. A murder of crows," he recites.

Haley just looks at him. "This is why people think you're weird," she finally says.

Lucas laughs. They walk for a moment. The smile fades from his face. "Sometimes I'd just like to show him what a mistake he made, you know?"

Haley doesn't miss a beat. "Dan?" she asks.

Lucas nods. "Mostly for Mom." He thinks. "And sometimes for me."

Haley understands. There's nothing to add. They walk on. Then she can't help asking. "So Luke, what are ravens? You know, more than one."

Lucas thinks. Smiles a thin smile. Looks at her. "An unkindness," he answers.

When he walks into the body shop a few minutes later, Keith puts him right to work. For a while, the two of them sink deep into what they're doing, Keith underneath one wreck and Lucas working on the fender of another. They've worked together long enough that they don't need to talk much, except to ask for tools or comment on a particularly nasty case of owner-attempted repair.

Finally, Keith pushes himself out from under the Toyota's chassis and asks the question he's been holding back since Lucas came in. "Why wouldn't you play?"

"I do play," Lucas says, picking up the conversation in midstream, without pausing. "I play every night."

"It's not the same, Luke," Keith says.

"Why?" Lucas looks honestly mystified. "What makes it less of a game if people don't see it?"

Keith's been thinking about this, and he's ready with an answer. "I'll tell you why." He gets up off the dolly, wipes off his hands on a rag. "When I was a kid my father took me to Raleigh to see David Thompson play. I'm nine years old, and I couldn't have cared less about basketball. So Thompson takes the court and, Luke" — he pauses, shaking his head at the memory — "he's young, and he's quick, and he's so graceful." Keith isn't even looking at Lucas. He's looking at something that happened a few decades ago. "Anyway," he goes on. "I was mesmerized."

Lucas is listening closely. Something about the way Keith is talking tells him that this is important.

"I couldn't take my eyes off him until late in the game," Keith continues. "And that's when I notice that my father is crying. Fourteen thousand strangers and my father has tears in his eyes. Because it was so beautiful. This kid who played the game with such poetry and made us feel like we were part of it."

Keith is smiling. The memory is so real that he can almost hear the roar of the crowd, smell the close smells of the packed field house. "You have a gift, Luke," he finishes quietly. "And it's a crime to rob people of the chance to feel that. To hide that inspiration in the park. It's a damn shame." He looks down at the rag he still holds. "That's why," he says at last.

They look at each other.

Then the phone rings. Keith wipes his hands again and goes to answer it. "Body shop and towing," he says.

*   *   *

Keith sends Lucas out on the call. It takes him about a half hour to get all the way out to the desolate country road where the caller was stranded. Lucas is glad for the time away from the shop. He needs a little while to digest what Keith has said.

When he rounds the bend and sees her car, it's like an electric surge in his body. Something that arises in his belly and zaps every other cell.

Peyton.

She's standing beside the Comet, sketchbook in her hand. Nothing registers on her face when she sees Lucas pull up in the wrecker.

Lucas steps out, approaches her. "That's me inside your head," he says.

"What?" She looks genuinely taken aback.

Lucas gestures at the sketchbook, which is covered in stickers. Among them is one displaying the NOFX band logo. "NOFX," Lucas says. "That's me inside your head. It's a lyric from —"

Peyton can't believe she missed the reference. It

must have been something to do with the shock of seeing him drive up, with the knowledge that the two of them were out there alone, on this quiet country road. "I know the song," she says, cutting him off.

Lucas nods and goes to the wrecker to pull out a clipboard. He starts filling out a towing order.

Peyton rummages for her cell phone, dials. "Nathan," she says into it, a moment later. "My car broke down, so you'll have to pick me up." She listens. "So practice is over. Get off your ass. . . ." She notices that Lucas is listening and walks off down the road a bit. "Look," she finishes. "It'll take you ten minutes. I'm on River Road near the curve." She listens again, frowns. "Yeah, well, it sucks to be you," she snaps, hitting the "end call" button.

She turns around to find Lucas handing her the clipboard for her signature.

"Sure you got a ride?" Lucas asks. He knows she doesn't. "I mean, I can wait if you want."

Peyton's in no mood. "Yeah," she says sarcastically. "That's what I want." She signs the form. "Just have your dad call me with the estimate."

"My uncle," Lucas corrects her.

Peyton raises an eyebrow. "If that's your story," she says drily, handing him the clipboard.

Right. Lucas takes it, heads for the cab of the truck. As he's stepping in, he calls back to her. "Hey, can I ask you a question?"

"Free country," Peyton answers.

"Why'd you become a cheerleader?" Lucas has a little grin playing at the corner of his mouth. "I mean, no offense, but you're about the least cheery person I know."

He climbs the rest of the way into the driver's seat. But he doesn't reach for the keys. Instead, he picks up his copy of *Julius Caesar* and starts to read, ignoring Peyton's glare.

She gives up and gets into the Comet, stubbornly hoping that Nathan will show up after all. She tries the ignition again. Nothing. Damn! She can't even crank some tunes while she's sitting here. Peyton flips open her sketchbook, pages through, sighs. It's all crap. She tosses the book into the backseat.

She gets out, slamming the door behind her, and starts to pace up and down the road. She checks her watch. Should she call Nathan again? Or would that just seem like begging?

Peyton. Sawyer. Does. Not. Beg.

Lucas watches her pace for a while. He has a nice view from the cab of the wrecker. Finally, he closes his book and steps out of the truck. "C'mon, you want a ride?"

Peyton pretends not to hear. She stares in the opposite direction.

"I'll let you insult me," Lucas says, in that same singsong voice kids use when they say, "I'll be your best friend."

Peyton almost smiles, hides it, lets him wait a few seconds. Then she walks over to him. "First of all," she says, counting on her fingers, "you don't know me." She glares at him. She didn't like that "least cheery" comment. "Second of all, you don't know me."

Now he's hiding a smile.

"Why are guys such jerks, anyway?" Peyton asks the universe.

"Guys?" Lucas asks. "Or Nathan?"

Ouch. He goes straight for the jugular, this one.

"Him," Peyton answers. "You."

"I don't know," Lucas says. Then, surprising himself, he adds, "We share the same father."

Wow! He actually said it. Peyton pretends not to react. "Yeah, I'd heard that," she says casually. "He's kind of an ass."

Lucas thinks of Dan. Now he's having a hard time hiding his grin.

"So," Peyton goes on, pushing it a little, "that must suck, seeing him around."

Lucas shrugs. "For my mom. I never knew him."

Peyton can't give up now. This is real stuff, from the source. "But she told you he was your dad," she probes.

"Eventually," Lucas answers simply. "We used to play in the junior leagues together. Me and Nathan." Why is he telling her all this?

"Basketball?" Peyton asks.

"Yeah," says Lucas. "I loved it." He looks right into her eyes, just for a heartbeat. "And I was good at it. You ever had something you knew you were better at than almost anyone else?" he asks.

"Sex," offers Peyton. "Joke," she adds quickly, when Lucas's eyes get wide. Is this getting a little deep, or what?

Lucas nods. "Anyway, the guys started teasing me about it. That Nathan's dad was mine, too. So I asked my mom and she said he wasn't. But when we got home I heard her crying in her room and I knew it was true."

Peyton is practically holding her breath. It's like if she said one syllable, he might stop. She doesn't want him to stop.

"So," Lucas goes on, "I never went back. I told my mom it was because I didn't want to have to see his face. But it was mostly because I didn't want her to have to."

By now, they've climbed into the truck. Peyton is

sitting next to him, staring out through the wind-shield. He hasn't started it up yet.

There's a brief silence. Then Peyton says, "Why'd you tell me that? We don't even know each other."

"Maybe that's the point," Lucas says, turning the key in the ignition.

Back at Scott's Body Shop, Keith is back under the Toyota. When he hears the bell on the front door ring, he figures it's Lucas, back from the wrecker call. "How'd it go?" he hollers. "Luke?"

No answer.

Keith emerges from the garage, wiping his hands on a rag, to find Dan standing in the office.

"How you been, big brother?" Dan asks. He manages to make the pleasantry sound smarmy, somehow sarcastic.

Keith manages to hide any surprise he feels at seeing his brother in his shop. "Not bad," he says, nodding. "You?"

"Good," Dan says briskly, as if talking to a

business acquaintance. "Dealership's good. I sent you some business not long ago."

Keith remembers. A lady with a dinged fender. One of those diddly jobs that takes longer than it's worth. "Yeah," he says. "I meant to call you and thank you for that."

"Well," Dan says magnanimously, "we're all busy, right?" Again with the businessman-to-businessman delivery.

Keith doesn't really know how to respond. It's obvious that Dan is here for a reason, but when's he going to get to the point? Keith has no patience with this dancing-around-the-subject bull. "So, what exactly can I do for you, Dan?" he asks.

Dan nods, as if it's predictable that his brother would be so blunt. "I wanted to talk to you about Karen's son," he says after a moment.

Keith recoils. "Karen's son," he repeats. He can't believe Dan said that. He feels like punching his smug, self-satisfied brother in his smug, self-satisfied stomach. But he controls himself. "Well, you should talk to Karen," he says, as calmly as he can.

Dan makes an impatient face, like Keith is wasting his time. "Nathan's got a real shot here, Keith. A real future." Doesn't his brother understand? It's not himself he's worried about. It's the boy.

But Keith doesn't, won't understand. "Yeah?" he asks. "And what about Lucas's future, Dan? You ever think about that?"

Dan just looks at him. He can tell that Keith hates him. Does he care? Not really. He puts on a calm, soothing tone of voice. "I can't change the fact that this boy exists," he says, carefully avoiding using Lucas's name. "If I could, I would. The truth is, I told Karen I'd take care of it, but she —" Suddenly, he stops speaking and looks past Keith to the front door.

Keith follows his eyes, and sees that Lucas has walked in.

How much did he hear? Keith holds his breath, wishing away Dan's presence.

But Lucas tosses the wrecker keys on the desk, grabs his basketball, and leaves without saying a word.

There's no doubt in either brother's mind. The boy heard everything.

*　　*　　*

Lucas dribbles the ball straight through the heart of town, taking the shortest route to the high school. When he gets there, he dribbles right on inside, and heads straight for the gym.

Nathan is in there, alone. Taking shots.

Lucas waits until Nathan stops to look at him.

"Tomorrow night," he says. "Midnight. At the river-front."

Nathan just nods.

"But if I win," Lucas says, "I'm gonna want something else."

Later that afternoon, it's Dan Scott who is surprised to find someone invading his turf. Karen has walked into his car dealership and seated herself in his office. She's staring calmly at a family portrait of Dan, Deb, and Nathan when he walks in, closing the door behind him. His heart is pounding. What does she want from him? He keeps his face impassive, even puts on his habitual smirk. "I'm guessing you're not car shopping."

Karen isn't there to beat around the bush. "He's a boy who wants to play basketball. Reluctantly," she adds. She's not smiling. "I find it horrifying and amusing that after all these years something as simple as that brings you around." She's talking about his visit to Keith.

"I'm just thinking of the kid," Dan says. Like it's all about what's best for her son.

Karen bristles. "Well, you have no right to think of him. Not today or any other day of his life. How dare you?"

Dan waits for her to wind down. "Are you finished?"

Karen looks disgusted. "I haven't even started. Since day one, we've asked nothing of you and you've delivered in fine fashion. I'll expect that to continue. If Lucas decides to play, you'll do nothing. Anything else might make me angry and detract from my pleasant, cordial side you're seeing right now." She gets up and starts walking toward the door.

"You know," Dan says thoughtfully, "I understand

your son doesn't exactly fit in." He sees her blink when he refers to the boy as hers, and knows he's getting to her. He goes on. "Nathan's All-State. I'm just not sure why you'd want to humiliate him like that."

Karen gives him a level look. "You're right, Dan," she says, not rising to the bait. "I'd rather not humiliate him. You've done that enough."

With that, she walks out the door.

October 19

"Nothing except a battle lost can be half so melancholy as a battle won."

—Duke of Wellington (1769–1852)

I'm not even sure what this quote means, but I have a feeling I may understand it better by later tonight – one way or the other. I don't honestly know whether I'll win or not, but I am beginning to know one thing: I do want to win. If nothing else, for Mom.

entry, Lucas's journal

WARM-UP: STRETCH HAMSTRINGS, CALVES, ACHILLES, QUADS, LOWER BACK (30 MIN EXTRA STRETCHING – GET LOOSE FOR TONIGHT.
SLOW RUN: 2 MILES – DON'T PUSH IT.
SPRINTS: NO SPRINTS TODAY. FOOTWORK DRILLS.
STRENGTH TRAINING (LIGHT DAY – JUST ENOUGH TO GET PUMPED):

STRAIGHT LEG DEADLIFT, BACK EXTENSION, BENCH PRESS, INCLINE CHEST FLY, BICEPS CURLS, FRENCH PRESS, WRIST CURLS, SQUATS, LUNGES, ABDOMINALS.
SHOOTING DRILLS: LAYUP, JUMP SHOT, THREES. LUCKY DRILL: SHOOT UNTIL HAVE MADE 13 IN A ROW.

entry, Nathan's training diary

Over at Nathan's, the atmosphere is tense. Game time is getting closer, and Dan is pacing the halls. He nearly bumps into Nathan coming out of the shower. "Hey, Dad," says Nathan. Quickly, he slings a towel around his neck.

Not quickly enough. Dan lifts the towel and spots the hoop through Nathan's pierced left nipple. "You know," he says cuttingly, "if I wanted a daughter I'd adopt one."

Nathan comes right back at him. "What, and abandon her, too?"

Dan's only reaction is a tightening of the jaw, a narrowing of the eyes.

It's enough to send Nathan stepping backward,

holding up his hands. "It's just a joke," he says. His dad is on overdrive tonight, even more intense than usual.

"And this bet tonight?" Dan asks. "Is that just a joke, or would you really quit the team? Because, let's be honest. You have everything to lose and nothing to gain."

Nathan just shakes his head. Does his dad ever see things from his point of view? If only his mom were here. She'd calm him down a little. "But sometimes," Nathan says carefully, "what you call everything I call nothing."

Dan tries another tack. "I just think it's best if you don't do this," he says, trying to sound reasonable. "We'll find another way."

"No," says Nathan. "I do a lot of stuff for you, Dad. Almost everything." He meets Dan's eyes. "But I'm doing this for me." He walks off down the hall.

Dan just stands there watching his son walk away. Finally, he turns to head down to the den. Just as he passes the bathroom door, Peyton pops out, a towel wrapped demurely around her.

At the cafe a few hours later, the dinner rush is over and the CLOSED sign is up. Karen and Keith are sorting through books, getting ready to fill some new shelves he's helping her hang. There's tension in the air, strange for the two of them who are normally so comfortable together. Finally, Karen breaks the silence. "So, I would've preferred a little warning shot on this one," she says. "Something to let me know what was coming with Lucas."

Keith nods. He knows she has a point. He shouldn't have gone to Whitey without telling her. And he should have let her know sooner about that night's one-on-one contest. "Fair enough," he admits. "I should have talked to you first. But you should see him play, Karen. It's poetry." He holds up a book of Robert Frost poems.

Karen lets out a huge sigh.

"Karen," Keith says. "He's gonna be fine."

She sighs again. "Yeah, I know. But . . ." She looks up at him. "You ever wonder about it, Keith? How we got to this?"

Keith grins, breaking the mood. "You mean, hanging out in a converted bookstore, lamenting the past, Haley listening in from the back?"

From the kitchen comes a voice. "I wasn't listening!" Then Haley appears at the serving window. "Okay, I was. I am." She grins and disappears again.

Keith reaches up to put a book away. "I wonder how we got to it so fast," he says, finally answering Karen's question.

"Oh, I don't know," Karen says. "When I see Lucas in high school, it seems more like the blink of an eye. But otherwise . . ." Her voice drifts off as she thinks back. "It seems like it's been forever."

"Forever since what?" Keith asks, even though he knows exactly what she's talking about.

"Since all of it," Karen says, after a moment.

Haley finishes up in the kitchen and heads up onto the roof, figuring she might find Lucas up there. Sure enough, he's lurking near one of the mini-golf holes, the one with the Smurf family figurines. She walks over to a switch and hits it. The whole place brightens, lit up by strings of sparkly white Christmas lights.

Lucas is surprised. "Wow," he says. "Looks nice!"

"Yeah, I just finished stringing the lights today. It's come a long way since we built that first hole," Haley says.

Lucas looks around, nodding.

Haley can tell his mind is on the night's duel. But he's not going to bring it up. "Your mom's worried," she reports. "She's downstairs with Keith, picking through her past."

Now Lucas is over by the roof railing, looking out at the lights of Tree Hill. "You think I'm being selfish by playing Nathan?" he asks. He can say anything to Haley.

"Why?" she counters. "Do you?"

Nathan is forced to admit it. "A little bit," he says. "I mean, if I walked away, my mom wouldn't be worried now, would she?"

Haley doesn't answer. She picks up a putter and walks over to the third hole, the one with a Hello Kitty theme. She puts a ball on the tee and stands back to study the layout. "You know, Luke, I don't tell you stuff like this because it sounds weird, but" — she takes a practice swing — "you're a good guy and I'm glad we're friends, but you and your mom worry too damn much." She takes a shot and sinks it. Then she can't help going on. "And the way I see it," she offers, "you've got nothing to lose. 'Cause no matter what happens tonight, your mom and Keith and the guys aren't going anywhere."

She puts the putter down and looks straight at him. Then she smiles. "And neither am I."

Eleven forty-five. Peyton and Nathan head out of the house, toward Tim's waiting car.

"So," she asks, "if you're not doing it for your dad, why are you doing it?"

Nathan is tired of talking about it. He just wants to be out there on the court, doing what he does best. "You wouldn't get it," he says.

"I guess not," Peyton says. "I mean, so what if this guy joins the team. Are you that threatened?" She knows she's pushing Nathan's buttons.

"I'm not threatened by anyone," Nathan says.

"Then why do it?" Peyton keeps pushing.

Nathan looks at her. Isn't it obvious? "To prove I'm the best," he says simply.

By then, they've reached Tim's car. Nathan reaches for the door handle. But Peyton has one more question.

"And what if he wins?" she asks. "What does he get?"

Nathan looks straight at her. "You."

Down at the river court, the fans are flooding into the park. It's a party! Music pours from a parked car and it looks as if half the school has turned out. Lucas is out on the court, trying to ignore the scene. But his concentration is off. He shoots and misses. Skills grabs the ball and fires it back, swallowing a smile.

Mouth and Edwards are in their element, playing to the crowd. This is the big time! "Just moments before the stroke of twelve," Mouth intones into his mic, "and still no Nathan Scott."

Edwards is wired. "And the natives are getting

restless, Mouth," he adds, "judging by the crowd that envelops our booth."

Junk rolls his eyes. "You don't have a booth," he informs his friends.

"Junk Moretti joins us now," Mouth says, as Junk joins them on the picnic table. "Junk, care to make a prediction?" He holds the mic toward Junk.

"Sure," says Junk. "I predict you guys'll be the two biggest morons out here."

Just then, the crowd volume rises audibly. Mouth cranes his neck. "And it looks like Nathan Scott has arrived, driven by car right onto the court," he reports.

Sure enough, Tim has pulled right onto midcourt.

"Believe that's a Honda Accord, Mouth," Edwards comments.

When the car has stopped, Nathan pops the door and climbs out, swaggering a little. The crowd erupts into cheers.

Tim jumps out and grins at Nathan. "Oh, by the way," he says. "Hope you don't mind, but I told a few people."

Peyton climbs out, too. Shooting a look at Lucas, she walks over to join Brooke on the sidelines.

Nathan grabs a ball out of the backseat and puts on a little dribbling exhibition. Then he bounces the ball off the backboard, leaps high, and slams the thing.

The crowd loves it.

Then there's a blast as Edwards leans into the airhorn. Tim pulls his car off the court, leaving center stage to the gladiators. Nathan and Lucas stand in the key, staring at each other as if they're the only two people for miles.

"You ready for this?" Nathan asks.

"Why not?" says Lucas.

"It's your life," Nathan says, dropping the ball at Lucas's feet.

"Yeah," says Lucas. "It is." He picks up the ball, and Nathan spreads his feet and his hands, ready to defend.

"Okay, folks," says Mouth. "Here we go. Fifteen by ones. Make it, take it, win by one. And you can feel the intensity in the air."

Edwards coughs. "Sports cliché," he says.

On the court, Lucas checks the ball to Nathan. Then he rotates it, lingering a little on the moment. He looks over at the crowd, meets Skills's eyes. Skills gives him a nod.

"C'mon," says Nathan. "Let's see it."

Lucas pulls up and lets go of a twenty-five footer. Swish.

"Oh!" Mouth yells. "A twenty-five footer rips the silk like Jimmy Edwards in a size-three dress!"

"Size six in dresses," Edwards corrects him, "twelve in pumps."

Behind them, Tim looks at an ex-teammate and shrugs.

Nathan grabs the ball and slings it back to Lucas, then drops back into his defensive stance. "Go ahead," says Nathan. "I'll give you that all night."

Lucas just blinks at him. Then he pulls up and sinks another.

"Luke drains another one," announces Mouth, "and it's two-zip, Lucas."

Tim frowns. "C'mon, Nathan. Go out on that."

Nathan retrieves the ball again, but he won't budge from his spot. Pride.

Lucas pulls up again. Buries it again.

The crowd is buzzing.

That's it. Nathan gives him the ball again, but this time he crowds right up next to Lucas.

"What happened to all night?" Lucas asks. He starts to dribble, putting the ball on the floor for the first time. He drives for the basket, only to have Nathan swat his layup into the crowd.

"Yes!" Tim says, throwing a fist in the air.

Nathan smiles, and the crowd responds. Then Nathan tosses the ball back to Lucas. "That all you got?" he asks.

Lucas takes a second to steel himself. Then he puts the ball on the floor again, spinning into the lane. Nathan smacks the ball away, stealing it. "Because if that's all you got," Nathan goes on, "this is over." With that, he slashes through the lane, shoots, and scores.

"Wow," says Edwards. "Nice drive. This looks to be a battle, Mouth."

"Sports cliché number two for the evening," says Mouth.

"Damn," says Edwards.

The game seems to go on forever. First one brother is up, then the other. Shot after shot sinks without a sound. It's a battle, and the crowd is loving it. Nathan is all over the court, showing off his drives and dunks. Lucas is shooting like a dream.

Finally, Nathan pounds the ball up the inside lane, blanketed by Lucas. Shoots. Scores.

"Thirteen to twelve," Mouth reports, "Nathan Scott with the lead as he bangs his way into the paint."

Lucas tries to stop him, but Nathan throws a shoulder into Lucas's chest. He spins hard, catching Lucas's nose with a vicious elbow thrust.

The crowd groans. It's like you can feel how much that hurt.

Lucas doesn't drop, but he bends at the waist. Blood drips onto the court. Meanwhile, Nathan goes ahead with a gimme layup. Lucas looks up at him, blood dripping down his face.

Skills, Fergie, and Junk are edging onto the court, ready to rumble.

So are Tim and the boys.

Then Haley pipes up. "You want me to beat his ass, Luke?" she yells from the sidelines.

That almost makes Lucas smile. He pulls up the bottom of his shirt and wipes off his face. Then he crouches down, ready to defend. "No foul," he says to Nathan. "Basket counts."

Nathan shrugs, deflecting the insult. He takes the ball.

"Besides," Lucas says, as Nathan checks the ball toward him. "You won't score again."

Nathan takes the ball back and chuckles.

"So," says Mouth, "the basket counts and it's fourteen-twelve, game point for Nathan. He could win it all right here."

Nathan fakes left and darts right. Lucas is all over him. Nathan backs off and works a crossover dribble, setting Lucas up. He fakes left. When Lucas leans, Nathan darts right. He's past Lucas in a flash, and he has a straight shot to the basket.

"Nathan for the win," Mouth sputters.

Nathan leaps. He lets go of a sweet finger roll that looks as true as they come. But before it reaches its height, Lucas rises and pins it against the backboard. He grabs it away as the crowd gasps audibly.

"Holy crap!" Mouth yells. "Did you see that? Someday men will write stories about that block. Children will be named after it. Argentinean women will weep for it."

Lucas pulls up and nails a jumper.

"Luke with the jumper," Mouth crows. "And that's as pretty as a blond on prom night."

Edwards nods happily. "New dress, hair pinned up, probably been to the tanning salon . . ."

Nathan retrieves the ball and hands it off to Lucas. "Down by one," he says, with an evil, thin smile. "Don't choke now."

Lucas doesn't answer. Not with words, anyway. He just pulls up and buries another long jump shot.

Mouth shouldn't be surprised — he's watched Lucas play for years — but his jaw drops. "Another dagger," he cries, "and it's all tied up!"

Edwards can't stand the tension. Or the clichés. "I think I'm gonna puke," he says.

Mouth just ignores him. "And I say this, Jimmy Edwards, Lucas Scott's stroke is all that was once pure and true and all that could be again!"

"Puking here," Edwards reports.

The crowd is going totally insane. Nathan goes for the ball and then stands there with it for a moment, his hands on his hips. He stares at Lucas. There's something in his eyes, something unfamiliar. Is it fear?

"C'mon, Nate," Tim yells. "Take him down."

Then, all sound seems to fade away. Lucas glances off court. At Peyton.

Nathan checks the ball. Starts to say something. Stops. Then he lets it out. "You know," he says quietly to Lucas. His brother. "You know, he's never mentioned you."

Nobody hears but Lucas.

But Lucas doesn't answer.

Nathan won't let it go. "He's never mentioned

you," he says again. "Not once in all these years." He comes in tight, grinning. Lucas won't get another jumper past him.

"This is for my mom," Lucas says. He fakes a shot. Goes right. Spins left. Nathan is on him like white on rice. They're pounding on each other.

"Lucas works the ball inside, right, then left, swarmed by Nathan," Mouth says breathlessly.

Edwards closes his eyes. "I can't watch."

Lucas backs Nathan down. Again. And again.

Then he fakes right and spins left into a fade-away jump shot.

Nathan lunges.

The shot is away, sailing toward the basket.

"Luke for the win —" Mouth roars.

"Ahhhhhh!" cries Edwards.

The shot is the most beautiful thing anyone in the crowd has ever seen. They're silenced by it.

"And it's GOOOOOD!" Mouth croons.

Half the crowd erupts in cheers. The other half? They seem to slump, like snowmen on a sunny day.

"Lucas Scott takes it fifteen-fourteen," Mouth cries, "and there is bedlam and delirium and felicity for all. . . ."

Skills rushes the court, followed by the other guys. They head for Lucas, ignoring Nathan, who boots the ball as he stalks off the court, head lowered. Nathan barely notices Peyton, who is standing in his path. He dodges her and keeps going.

She lets him.

After a moment, Lucas sees her standing there. He steps away from his friends, walks over to her.

"So," she asks, trying to keep her voice from trembling. "What did you bet?"

Lucas meets her eyes. He knows what she thinks. "I win," he says. "Nathan stays on the team."

Peyton's eyes widen. She didn't expect that. "Why?"

"Because it's the last thing he wants," Lucas tells her. "And anyway, it's not about him. It's about me."

Over near Tim's car, Nathan is watching. "Peyton," he says.

Peyton gives Lucas one more look. Then she turns and heads toward Nathan.

Lucas stands there, watching her walk away. "I'll be seeing you," he says to her back.

Peyton slows down for a moment. She looks back at him. Then she moves on.

When Nathan arrives home, he finds his father waiting up. Dan is sitting slumped in an easy chair, a glass of whiskey on the side table next to him. He looks up hopefully when Nathan walks in. Nathan meets his father's eyes. "Don't worry, Dad," he says, "your dreams are still safe."

For a split second, Dan's eyes light up. Could this mean that Nathan won? Then they cloud over again as he registers the sarcastic tone in his son's voice.

When Lucas comes up the walk, he spots Karen sitting on the porch swing. As he comes up the stairs, she stands and opens her arms, offering him her loving embrace. Winner or not, she adores him.

"I won," he mumbles into her shoulder.

She holds him even tighter.

Later, upstairs, Lucas sits looking at his computer. His browser is now set to open on Peyton's web page and rarely goes anywhere else. He tries to calm himself by reading from *Julius Caesar*. But he stops every few seconds to check Peyton's image. She's working at her desk — drawing, of course. There's something in the furrow in her brow, the set of her mouth. She looks . . . vulnerable. Lucas feels a twinge deep in his belly, and goes back to Shakespeare.

" 'There is a tide in the affairs of men,' " he reads, " 'which, taken at the flood, leads on to fortune; omitted, all the voyage of their life is bound in shallows and miseries. On such a full sea are we now afloat, and we must take the current when it serves, or lose our ventures.' "

Lucas puts the book down and takes one more look at Peyton. Then he turns off the light and goes to sleep.

Epilogue

Whitey stands, arms folded, watching as what's left of his Ravens warm up with a skip pass shooting drill. Five balls are bouncing at once as another, tossed by Nathan, swishes through the net. Across the gym, Peyton, Brooke, and the other cheerleaders practice a new step. Business as usual — except that everybody keeps glancing at the door, as if they're waiting for someone to arrive.

Then he does.

Lucas steps into the gym.

The shoot-around stops.

Brooke freezes in midstep.

The lines from *Julius Caesar* are still playing in Lucas's mind as he gazes around.

" 'And we must take the current when it serves, or lose the ventures before us . . .' "

The Scott brothers look at each other.

Nathan, the king in his castle.

Lucas, at the end of a journey into a new world.

And Peyton, somewhere between them.

Something has to give in this place called Tree Hill.